Limitations

Limitations

By Aimee J Edwards

Aimee J Edwards

5

This book is dedicated to all who dare to dream.

Prologue

Dear Lilly,

You're young… too young. You can't imagine anything worse than the repercussions of being out of bed earlier than allowed. A plane flies into a building, the glass shatters, a pillar of strength crumbles to the ground as a car races away. You're alone now, left to pick up the pieces of a broken life, but what happens when you don't? Twenty years later, what remains? Anxiety, fear and self-doubt control your life, squandering any potential that ever threatened to shine through. You are the bird that burned alive over and over

Limitations

and over again while all the other phoenixes rose from the

ashes. This is your life, are you going to fight for it?

From Lilly

Chapter 1

Walking through Harlem, breathing in the pre-summer air, I was transported back to my happy place, and for a few moments, I was at peace. Then a siren started to ring out, and suddenly, violently, I was pulled back to reality.

It was nearing 10pm by the time I arrived home from work at the convenience store. Mum was still up, sitting on the couch and reading through paperwork.

"Hey, Mum," I said softly as I walked in the door.

"Hello, darling," Mum sung back to me. "How was work?"

"Excruciatingly long." I exhaled sharply.

Limitations

In the kitchen, I grabbed some leftover Chinese takeout from the fridge, and moved to the microwave to reheat it. That's when I saw it – the pamphlet on the kitchen counter: "9/11 Forgotten Survivors – it's time to overcome what's holding you back" it proclaimed in bold white lettering.

My mother, ever the puppeteer, had been leaving these brochures around the house for weeks. She had found it on a notice board at a medical appointment. Deciding that it was the only thing that could possibly help me, she would not rest until I agreed.

I wouldn't exactly say I have the best mental health. I mean, I can't leave the house without checking if I've turned my hair straightener off at least five times. I can turn something as mundane as putting the trash out into a terrifying scenario that almost always ends in my untimely and brutal death. No one has ever been able to help – the fear and anxiety rages on just as strong as ever – so why put myself through all the pain of getting my hopes up and having them torn back down?

"Mum," I snapped at her, "how many times do I have to tell you? I'm not doing this stupid program!"

Mum stood up, exasperated. "Why not, Lilly?" she snapped.

"Because it's complete and utter nonsense," I yelled, then read the brochure in a condescending tone, "Broaden the scope of your potential. Don't let fear and worry hold you back any longer." I laughed. "I mean, really? Could that sound any more made up?"

My mother is somehow the most intelligent and most gullible person I have ever met. I don't for the life of me know how she got that way. She's a lawyer, trained to question everything. But at home, she breathes new life into the concept of leaving work at the office – she'll believe just about anything!

Limitations

"All I'm saying is, you can't spend the rest of your life in a dead-end job just waiting for inspiration to strike," Mum said sternly.

"It's a means to an end at this point, Mum," I replied. We have had this same conversation so many times. I didn't have the strength to go through it all again.

"Lilly!" Mum yelled back. "I supported you when you told me you didn't want to go to college. I supported you while you wasted every single opportunity you have been given, but I am just about at my quota for support."

We have been doing this dance, back and forth, for months now. Mum doesn't think I put enough time into making something of myself, mostly because she doesn't know the extent of the troubles that plague my mind on a daily basis. I honestly just wish she'd leave me alone.

"Lilly, I moved us all the way here to give you a better life, to get you away from all that destruction. You were the top of your grade, voted most likely to succeed, and here you are, twenty-five and working in a convenience store, without a degree to your name. Is it so bad that I want more for you?" Mum said.

"Really? You brought me here for a better life?" I snapped back, sarcastically. "That's funny – all these years I thought you brought me here to keep me away from Dad. But I am so very glad it was all for me."

"Lilly, that isn't fair." Mum's voice was earnest.

"None of this is fair, Mum. For the eight hundredth time, would you please just leave me alone!? I'll work it out when I work it out."

"Fine. I'll leave you alone, but this isn't normal, Lilly. You need help, you need to stop ignoring every professional you see. I want you to have a life that you're proud of ... not this."

"No, Mum," I yelled, "you want me to have a life that you're proud of." I stormed out of the kitchen and into my bedroom, slamming the door behind me.

Limitations

I wished I could say my mother was wrong, but sadly she was not. I had wasted every opportunity I had been given. I had told her I would just take a gap year and go to college soon, but soon came and left, and here we were, eight years out of high school and not a single college credit to show for it. It's not like I didn't want more for myself, but I just didn't have enough faith that I was capable of it. So, I kept a job that paid the bills and kept my head down, hoping that no one around me noticed how much I was struggling. The truth was that I was afraid to start something new because I was afraid of failure. I was afraid that if things fell apart, as they always did, I wouldn't be able to put myself back together again. My grandfather died the year after I finished school. He suffered for a really long time, so I knew it was for the best, but it broke me. We were close, and it broke every little part of me to know that the constant in my life for so long was no longer with us. Every fear and anxiety that resided beneath the surface broke free, and suddenly, it was like I didn't remember how to take a breath anymore without fearing it would be my last. When the phone rang, I waited for the news that would shatter my whole world all over again. I suffered while others thrived, and every day was a battle to keep my mind out of the dark places –to keep my head above water. Mum wanted me to have a better life, but I was just fighting to stay alive.

The first time I felt that way, I was five years old. I was early on a chilly winter's morning in Sydney, Australia, and I decided that I had slept enough. So, I rolled, stealth-like, out of bed, army crawled over to my chest of drawers, opened the bottom draw, pulled out a small pink jumper with the words "skater girl" written in rhinestones across its front, and pulled it over my head. I want the record to show that I was not, in fact, a skater girl, but, boy, did I love that jumper as if I were one! With my jumper protecting my body from the cold, I continued my secret mission out of the bedroom, down the narrow hallway, past the dark kitchen and into the lounge room. Quietly, I rifled through cushions before finding the remote control and hitting the on button. I wasn't a dumb kid – I knew I wasn't allowed to be up that early, so, knowing that the picture would take approximately twenty seconds to appear on the screen, I used my waiting time to turn the volume all the way down to avoid blasting my parents out of their slumber. However, I did not get the chance to turn the volume back up when the picture finally came up on the screen. You see, instead of the expected image of Big Bird chattering to Elmo, I was faced with something completely different and much more sinister – a jumbo jet flying into the side of a building.

Without a single thought about how much trouble I would get in for being up so early, I screamed, at the top of my lungs, causing my mum to come running, half-dressed, into the living room. To my great surprise, when Mum saw the television, she screamed as well – just as loud as I had, if not louder. Up until that point, I was a little girl who believed the world was all good and the worst thing that could ever happen was that my mother might find me out of bed early. But, in an instant, I was thrust into a world were planes flew into buildings and there was nothing anyone could do to control it.

As I got older, I learnt to deal with the mess that my life had become. I was an overachiever who had to be the absolute best at everything I did, no matter what the cost. I lived for the happy moments but grew evermore concerned that something big, dark and scary was lurking just around the corner. For a few years, around high school, I settled into life; I accepted that sometimes bad things happened and there was nothing that I could do about them. I told myself I was fine, that I would survive. It's amazing how believable the lies we tell ourselves are when there is nothing to prove them wrong.

They say it's in our weakest moments that we learn just how strong we are. I disagree – in my weakest moments, every fear was realised, and I was not strong enough to make it through.

Mum didn't talk to me for a few days after our big blowout. She wasn't the most forgiving woman, and even if she had been, it wasn't exactly like I was going to apologise. I might have known I was wrong, but I sure as hell wasn't going to let her know that.

I hid out in my room, reading books and catching up on television shows, and only left to pick up a food delivery from the front door or to sneak to the bathroom. Two days later, as I headed out of my bedroom for a shift at work, I found myself face-to-face with Mum.

"Lilliana," she said abruptly.

A rage built inside me. I absolutely hated that name; it was written on my birth certificate, citizenship and passport and absolutely nowhere else. Lilliana was my great grandmother's name. I never met her, and as much as I like having that connection to someone Mum loved so much, when Mum uses that name, it sets off something inside me.

"Mother," I responded, sidestepping her and walking into the kitchen. I grabbed a bottle of orange juice from the fridge and quickly exited the apartment, leaving my mother ranting about something that was bound to have been complete nonsense.

The cute little convenience store, Ella Tienda, that had been my home away from home for quite a few years, was located in the closest underground subway stop to our home. Working underground as trains rattle past, I got used to the feeling of the earth shaking beneath me. But on this day, having read an article just that morning about the city of Christchurch, New Zealand, and the earthquakes that had flattened it just ten years ago, I was not prepared to feel the ground shake beneath me. I was stocking the shelves when it happened. The ground shook; the walls vibrated; and my heart rate rose to an unnaturally high level. I had had panic attacks before. I knew when they were coming on and I knew how to deal with them, but this was different. If the shop's owner, Matias, hadn't been there with a paper bag to help me calm down, I would have most definitely found myself in the nearest emergency room.

As I walked home later that afternoon, I made a decision that I was bound to regret in the days that followed, but for a few moments, actively choosing to get help felt good. Mum was smart; she knew what was best for me even if I didn't always want to admit it.

When I arrived home, I jumped online and signed up for the "Forgotten Survivors" program, which commenced in two weeks. I also sent an email to Matias, giving my two weeks' notice.

To her credit, there were no "I told you so's" when I told Mum later that night. Instead, she just smiled at me and whispered, "It's ok to accept help, Lilly. I'm glad you've finally realised that."

Honestly, I don't know if I had realised it. It wasn't my first therapy session, and I wasn't exactly what you would call optimistic about the program, but something needed to change.

I spent the next two weeks training a new staff member in the store and reading anything that would distract me from the inevitably doomed mission I was about to embark on.

By the time the sun rose on the morning of the first session, I was in full denial mode and any preconceptions that this might have been a good idea were drowned out by fear and anxiety.

Chapter 2

The room was a small rectangular office hidden in a forgotten part of the New York City Library, illuminated by a single flickering light bulb. The old but apparently effective air conditioning unit blew dust particles into the open space as the elderly female moderator and I sat in a circle of chairs, making awkward small talk. She was a short, stocky woman, probably in her late sixties, with short blonde hair that was almost definitely dyed to hide the grey hairs she had accumulated while working with crazy people like me. She wore small lmauve-framed spectacles that sat a little too low on the bridge of her nose for them to actually be doing any good. You know those people you see once, and you just know you don't like them? There is no reason for it or logic behind it – you just don't like them? Yep, she was one of them!

Typically, I would aim to arrive early – fifteen minutes before I had to. I would always leave home a little earlier than was needed just in case there was traffic or I ran out of money on my MetroCard or there was some other massive event that would stop me from getting somewhere on time. I guess that comes from living here most of my life – in New York City you are no stranger to unexpected delays. You learn to plan your life around them and how to deal with the wait when you arrive to your destination early.

That morning, I had used the subway. It was a twenty-minute trip from Harlem on the B train to the 42nd Street—Bryant Park subway stop, and then only a five-minute walk to the library. In peak-hour traffic, it could take almost triple that to drive – not that I had a car to drive. It

Limitations

was one of the easy days: I filled up my MetroCard the day before; the first train that came along had just enough space for me to squeeze in; and there were only a few dogs to pet in Bryant Park on my walk to the library.

The acid in my stomach churned and bubbled as unfamiliar bodies, with uncertain faces, entered the dark room and took a chair. Each one of them looked pained, like they had been brought down here against their will. I guess that's how I looked too. Realistically, who opts to spend four weeks delving into the deepest and darkest parts of their subconscious with a group of strangers in a freezing, poorly lit room in a 120-year-old library? Not a single soul – not for themselves anyway.

One by one, the other members passed the snack table lined with every sugary treat known to man and took their seats, each commencing with the same awkward small talk I had been engaged in up until now. A small upside –

their arrival gave me the ability to sink back into my chair, letting my mind drift away from the room.

I pictured myself on a long, white, sandy beach with water so blue that it was difficult to know where the sea ended and the sky began; my nose was buried in a book and the soft sea breeze blew my hair gently away from my face. Drifting into the book, I created my own endings in my head, coming up with stories for the characters outside of their existence in the book. I had always been this way – creative to the point that it annoyed the hell out of everyone around me. What they didn't get was that it was not some weird thing I did for fun, it was a coping mechanism. When it all got too much, it was easier to drift into someone else's life, a fictional life. It was not that I hated my life or anything, but sometimes, fiction was just easier to swallow than reality.

As the last member of the group entered and took the remaining seat, I was woken from my fantasy. The

Limitations

moderator rose to commence a four-week-long period of what was bound to be utter hell.

"Welcome to Forgotten Survivors. My name is Andrea," she declared, raising her arms to the room like she oversaw some huge cult. I paused for a second, pondering that thought. If anyone was going to get her daughter accidentally involved in a cult, it would be my mother. She was the smartest person I knew, but the woman was once convinced that the prince of Nigeria was desperately in love with her, and she would've transferred a decent sum of money to him if I hadn't ended the call before she got the chance. Does Nigeria even have a prince?

"Over the next four weeks we will be rebuilding you, reshaping the way you think and analysing the way you react in the face of trauma. Group therapy has helped thousands before you. You are united through your shared experiences and will guide each other on your path to a bright and hopeful future." Andrea spoke in a way that made you want to join her but also want to rip your ears off so you never had to hear her again. She was like the perfect combination of therapist and aggressive librarian, giving you the weirdest sense of genuine discomfort. As I looked around the room, I spotted a few thinly veiled eye rolls. I'm not sure a combined distain for her is what Andrea had in mind when she said, "shared experiences", but that seemed to be what was happening.

"Each day we will start with a story from one member of the group, and as a team, we will unpack that, connect through these experiences and develop ways to deal with our individual problems. It is our hope that this kind of deep investigation will teach you the skills you need to unpack your own mental-health struggles. On our twelfth day together, we will reflect on what we have learnt so far. Our aim is to teach you to deal with the things that are holding you back and help you move forward with your lives in the face of unspeakable tragedy."

Limitations

I didn't know if there was any substance to what this crazy-sounding woman was saying, but her message seemed to resonate with us all. The room had come to life in the slightest ways. Had anyone walked in at that moment, they would not have thought it was a lively room, but the exhalations, scuffle of feet, and cracking of necks were a welcome addition to the once uncomfortably silent room. I don't think that many of us wanted to be there, but I got the feeling that each one of us needed to be. We were all tempted by the thought of a brighter and better future.

Andrea continued her speech. I had decided, by that point, that I would at least show up to the next day of this program – in case, by some miracle, it worked better than all the others I had already gone through.

A tall, overweight man, probably in his early fifties, sat across from me. He certainly liked his donuts – he held two in one hand and was fiddling with the sprinkles on top.

His face was drawn and sunken, the bags under his eyes pushing everything below them down.

As Andrea droned on, I switched my gaze to another man, just two seats to the right. He was really built, with the body of a man who had spent every spare hour in the gym – hiding from something, perhaps? His legs were completely hairless, and on the surface, they looked rough, dry and discoloured, like meat that had been defrosted in the microwave just a little too long. The backpack at his feet was emblazoned with a familiar lettering and logo, "FDNY". That's when it all started to add up. He had been burnt in the line of duty, one would assume. I wondered if he was on site *that day*, if that was where the burns came from, if that was the reason he was here.

The next person along had one of those faces you can't help but notice. Had I seen him in any other circumstances, and had I not been completely closed off to any and all romantic ventures, I would have gone to extreme

Limitations

lengths to keep looking at him. He was tall, fit, with messy blonde hair that fell into his bright blue eyes. If I'm being perfectly honest, he was gorgeous, but that's not what made me notice him. There was something else about him that spoke to me. Of all the people in that room, he looked the most determined, the most certain. The expression on his face told me that he not only felt like he needed to be there, but that he wanted to be there.

I shook my head slightly and looked toward the man whose voice now filled the room.

It seemed we were now up to the thoroughly mortifying part of these sessions where we would go through our name, one random fact about ourselves and one thing we were hoping to get out of the program. This game had haunted schools and board meetings since the beginning of time. I used to think it was a way of intimidating the people in the group, a way of dwindling down the introverted until only the outgoing survived. I'm less naive now. Now I think it's just a way for the moderator to look like she's making progress. She gets our stories, hears our hopes and our dreams – it's all just another box to check off her list.

One by one, the group took it in turns naming themselves, giving just the slightest little snippet from their personal lives, and sharing the smallest portion of their hopes and dreams. Some told the group something funny or outrageous that had once happened to them. Some thought the most interesting thing they could possibly share about their lives was their favourite food or an anecdote about the time they sat near a celebrity on a plane, which is kind of sad if you think about it for too long. What struck me as simultaneously amusing and comforting was the repetition of one word when it got to the description of what we wanted out of the program. In all the aloof, vague answers, the word "change" seemed to be a motif throughout, hiding behind the thin veil of its synonyms. We all wanted a change and to see the world differently, and in that, I found comfort.

When Andrea started this exercise, she had gone clockwise starting to her left and going all the way around the circle before finally getting to me. The nine people before me had given me a chance to formulate the best possible answers, but I had squandered it. Then, as all eyes turned to me, I was frozen ... My stomach churned ... I took a deep breath, homing in on the conversations I had had with Mum that had led me there.

"Hi ... My name is Lilly. I am twenty-five years old. You didn't ask that, but there's a random bit of info for you. I was born in Australia and moved here when I was six. What I want out of this program? Um ... I guess, I just don't want to be afraid anymore."

Chapter 3

Doctors have this way they look at you when they're about to give you bad news. First, they look down, as if to ponder the implications of what they're about to say, then, in a move that catches you completely off guard, they blurt it all out. I often wonder if they ever fathomed the impact their words have.

I had been seeing therapists on and off since I was five years old, but the blow of their words never ceased to shatter the shield I had built around myself.

OCD, high-functioning anxiety, thanatophobia, situational depression, PTSD, insomnia, anhedonia. The list goes on and on, an ever-tightening noose around my neck. The reality of labels is, the more you have, the harder it becomes to identify yourself. You start to make lists of them all in your phone, making sure that each new doctor is aware of everything you've been told before. You start to become the diagnoses and the human behind them fades away. I don't know how accurate any of mine are. Some I have laughed about. Some I have cried over. Some have confused the hell out of me. But each diagnosis takes up permanent residence in my mind – a reminder that, for me, normality will always be an unreachable destination.

On the way home from the first meeting as the train rattled violently along the tracks, I thought about the people I had just left. Every seemingly insignificant detail of their appearance, and the way they held themselves, told a story. I couldn't imagine any of them struggling with the first assignment. I could imagine each of them returning home, making dinner or doing their taxes, just getting on with their lives, and coming back the next day, ready to tell their story unapologetically. Oh, to be that sure of one's self.

In the past, my therapy sessions had been guided. There was always some grey-haired man or woman telling me I felt this way because of this or that way because of that. They told me what was wrong, and I added it to my ever-growing list. But this time, I was completely on my own, and repeating a second-hand diagnosis wouldn't cut it.

As the train approached my station, I jumped to my feet, slung my handbag over my shoulder and disembarked through a crowd of people heading into the city for the evening. I rushed through the crowd and toward the station exit before changing course and entering Ella Tienda.

As I walked through the store entrance, happy memories flooded my mind. The owners cared about their staff and were passionate about helping their community. It had been a good job, but I wanted more and there had been times where it drained all life out of me. Despite my boss saying my job would always be open, I hoped that I wouldn't have to return.

I grabbed a bottle of Vanilla Coke out of the fridge and a family-sized Hershey's Cookies and Cream bar off the shelf and paid at the front counter. If I was going to play Dr Frankenstein, reassembling fragments of my past, sugar and caffeine were the only things that might help me through it.

"How are you feeling, Lilly?" Matias, the shop owner, yelled out to me from the back of the store.

"Keeping on keeping on, Matias. Paciencia y fe," I yelled back before grabbing my items and exiting the store. This handy little aphorism means "patience and faith". I'd like to pretend I learnt it from school or extensive time working in the community, but, if I am being completely honest, it came from a musical.

When I finally exited the muggy station, I paused for a moment, taking a deep breath in through my nose and out through my mouth. This was something my mum taught me to do when I was younger, to help me cope when things all felt a little too much. "If you are still alive and you can still breathe for yourself, nothing can really be that bad" she would say with a slightly condescending smile. It shouldn't work, but for whatever reason, it often managed to stop me from spiralling out of control.

Feeling somewhat alive for the first time that day, I reached into my bag, removed my AirPods and hit shuffle on my favourite Apple Music playlist. I strolled through the streets of uptown New York, timing each step perfectly with the beat of "Someone Saved My Life Tonight" by Elton John, which was playing in my ear. The city raced past me, commuters headed to subway stations, locals headed out to dinner, cars tried to get from point A to point B, and I continued, trying desperately to shut them all out.

By the time I arrived home, the streetlights had made their presence known and an eerie blackness filled every corner of our small apartment. When I say small, I

Limitations

don't mean it conventionally. In comparison to other apartments in New York it was quite spacious, but any time someone from back in Australia came to visit, they gawked at its size, shocked by the "unreasonable" price we paid for it. New York City is notoriously expensive. It's one of the main reasons I still live at home. It's too expensive to live in this city alone, and despite everything, I wouldn't want to live anywhere else.

We first moved here from Australia when I was six. Life had been crazy in the year leading up to the move. I was scared of my own shadow and this impacted everyone around me. Dad gave up pretty quickly. He was never really one to accept any form of challenge, always in pursuit of the "simple life". After they split, Mum needed a change. That house, that suburb, the entire city reminded her of everything she had lost. So, she quit her job in Sydney, called in a favour with an old friend in New York and we were on a plane to the Big Apple within a year of 9/11.

When I say "they split", it wasn't exactly like they sat down, had a mature discussion and made an amicable decision. Dad screamed, Mum cried, and I hid under my bed. I heard Dad's car start, then it screeched down our suburban street, and in an instant, we became a family of two. I have only seen my dad once since that day: I was sixteen, back home to see the family for Christmas break, and he was waiting in line at the local fish and chip shop. I watched him from afar as he ordered a family-sized chips, and then, when it was ready, he walked straight past me without so much as a nod in my direction. It hurt – he didn't recognise his own daughter! But it hurt even more to know that, somewhere, he would be sharing those chips with another family, a whole family that my mother and I would never be a part of.

Standing in the doorway, I reached my arm inside and hit the light switch to illuminate our home. Mum wouldn't be home for hours. As a big hotshot lawyer, she

Limitations

often worked late into the night. Honestly, I admired her for it – the passion that she channelled into helping people and seeing justice served – it's something I longed for but could never quite find. I spent so much of my childhood blaming my mum for making us leave Australia, and there are moments when I still do, but in all that hurt and blame, I often forget to tell her that she makes me proud every single day.

I opened Uber Eats on my phone and ordered a ham and cheese pizza from a local Italian restaurant. A large would be enough to get me through a night's worth of soul-searching with some left over for Mum's late-night snack when she finally arrived home. We weren't exactly gourmet chefs in my house. I don't mind a bit of baking here and there, and we are actually not half-bad cooks when we try, but we are usually too exhausted to bother.

By the time the delivery driver arrived at the front door with dinner, I was already buried in piles of paperwork

– information sheets, peculiar drawings scribbled on the back of scrap paper and receipts – that I hoped they would spark my memory. I jumped at the sound of the knock, and it all spilled across the floor. Grunting and groaning, I made my way through the mess and toward the front door, almost tripping on a box of old letters that now sat in the entrance to my bedroom.

It was hours and several episodes of *Grey's Anatomy* later before I finally returned to my mission for answers. I stood in the doorway of my bedroom, staring down at the box of letters. In the early days, a psychologist had suggested I write letters to myself to help me understand the way I was feeling and as an outlet for the emotions that had been suffocating me. It was one of the few things that ever really stuck. I added a new letter every few weeks. The content wasn't exactly revolutionary – all it seemed to do was take some of the weight off my chest. I bent down and picked up a dusty envelope with 03/03/2012 written on the front of it. Inside, my messy writing seemed to scream at me

from the creased paper.

Dear Lilly,

He doesn't love you. No one ever will. He proved that over and over again when he made fun of you for feeling the way you did. He'd say, why can't you just pull yourself together? It's pathetic that you are still crying over this. He's not worth the tears you've cried for him.

You just got 96% in an English literature assignment and you have the One Direction concert this weekend. Get over yourself and keep smiling.

From Lilly

I was thankful that my writing had developed over the years and that I had my priorities a little more in order. That being said, I would have liked to go back to a time when all the dark and scary parts of life could be overshadowed by an upcoming One Direction concert. With a loud bang, my thoughts were pulled away from goofy boys with cheeky smiles and tight pants.

"Lilly! You're still up?" said my visibly drained mother. "How was the day?" She plodded into the kitchen, dropped her things on the bench and filled a glass to the brim with Sauvignon Blanc.

"Oh … it was certainly a day," I dismissed with a laugh. "I have all this work to do before tomorrow, but it's just not happening for me. How was your day?" I asked, desperate to pull the attention away from me.

Limitations

"Oh, you know," she said, "same shit, different day. Some crackpot judge trying to tell me I don't know what I'm talking about. I might have considered his point if the defendant's lawyer wasn't one of his old frat-party mates."

Katherine Dempsey, my mother, was a staunch feminist, much like myself, but she took it to the extreme. Anything that went wrong in her life she would blame on the patriarchy and turn it into some big campaign for equal rights and pay. I could have used this as my out, I could've taken advantage and got her all riled up until she forgot that today was different to any other, but it wasn't worth the effort.

"Bloody men," I said. "So, tomorrow, I have to explain the reason I'm in therapy … I mean, isn't that just ridiculous? It's like going to a doctor and explaining why I'm sick. Isn't that someone else's job to work out?" I laughed awkwardly before grabbing her wine bottle and pouring a glass for myself.

Mum rolled her eyes, grabbing the bottle out of my hands. Her expression screamed, "Do you really think that is going to help?" Then she took the bottle back to the fridge.

"Sweetheart, this is the reason we are doing this," she said.

I glared at her over the rim of the glass, sipping what I was permitted to drink.

"I know it's not easy to face the things that haunt you, but that doesn't mean it's not important." She looked deep into my eyes as she spoke.

I sighed because deep down I knew she was right, even if I didn't want it to be true.

"I know. That's why my room looks like it was hit by a tiny hurricane. I'm going through every part of my therapy to date and analysing it … It's all a bit overwhelming," I replied with an exasperated exhale.

Limitations

"Just keep plugging away – the answers will come to you. They have to be in there somewhere or you wouldn't feel the way you do." Mum sighed with a smile.

"Yeah … I'm going to get back to it," I said, sculling what was left in my wine glass before placing it in the kitchen sink. "There's some pizza in the fridge if you're hungry. I'll be in my room."

"I'm glad to see you trying, sweetheart," Mum called out.

I stepped over the box of letters and closed the door behind me.

My mother was the kindest, most compassionate person I have ever met, and she tried, she really did, but a part of me always felt like she never fully understood.

Most of the time it was like I was an alien being observed by humans, and no matter how hard they tried, they just couldn't quite understand me. But then, for a brief moment, a line of a book or the lyrics of a song or a piece of dialogue in a television series make me feel seen. Those are the moments that I feel most alive.

About three-quarters of the way through the pile of paperwork, with no further idea of what was going on inside my head, I officially gave up. Sitting in the middle of my bed, surrounded by mess on all sides, I looked up at myself in the mirror on the wall and nodded.

With my hands and feet, I began pushing everything off the bed onto the carpeted floor, telling myself I would clean it up in the morning. I put on an old Ed Sheeran concert shirt and TJ Maxx bed shorts, climbed into bed and buried myself under the covers.

As my eyes closed, my mind flicked through the events of the day. I remembered old therapy sessions and noted that I felt at least somewhat different tonight than I did after those. My eyes opened suddenly with the realisation that I hadn't said goodnight to my mother. I grabbed my phone out from under my pillow and sent a quick text, *Good night, love you.* I realise how completely neurotic this is, but in my head, if I didn't say good night and if I didn't say I love you, something horrible might have happened in the middle of the night, and it would be entirely my fault. I know, I know, I'm completely mental.

After hours spent tossing and turning – as was a common occurrence for me – I finally drifted to sleep. My dreams were filled with dark figures in the night, hiding in the shadows of unstable buildings. Ghosts taunting me as they watched the world go by without them.

At 7am, the sound of my alarm going off under my pillow was a welcome surprise, a jerk into the light once more. I lay staring at the ceiling, my heart pounding loudly in my chest at the thought of returning to the support group today. I searched for some excuse to stay in bed for the foreseeable future, but nothing came.

When the alarm rang out again, marking ten minutes since it first went off, I pulled myself out of my trance and slowly out of bed. The city was just waking up and I would have given anything to hide in my room for the rest of the day. But the universe had other plans, I may not have been ready for day two, but it was sure as hell ready for me.

Chapter 4

There are so few moments in life when we can say that everything went exactly according to plan, but there are many when the universe truly feels like it is in control of your destiny. From the traffic that makes you late for an appointment to the call that runs overtime and puts you far enough away from a huge accident. A few years back, my best friend Ella had been on a trip to Florida and had made a last-minute decision to stop at a McDonalds before starting her big night of partying at Pulse Nightclub. She was standing up to leave when she got a news alert on her phone announcing that a gunman had opened fire at the venue and that there were multiple fatalities. Ella didn't even bother to return to her hotel that night; she got a taxi straight to the airport and flew home. In the days that followed, we learnt that forty-nine innocent lives were lost inside that club and hundreds more would never be the same again. One decision and I may have never seen my best friend again. One decision that every one of those people inside that club could have made. But there was no way to know which decision was the right one, no way to know when you were damning or saving yourself. It's these moments, that make me want to believe in a higher power. I think you have to believe that there is some grand plan, or I would be swallowed by the randomness of it all. In the wake of that event, Ella kept moving, she used her new-found knowledge of the fragility of life to drive her forward while I stayed behind, still fighting my own demons.

In my heart, I knew day two was not going to go according to plan, and my suspicions were proven correct as

Limitations

I arrived at the overcrowded subway station. I had allowed myself one hour to make the twenty-minute trip downtown. Seven trains had passed since arriving, each of them so packed that I couldn't squeeze in even, if I had the desire to live like a sardine for the next twenty minutes. It seemed like every human being in Harlem and their dog had decided to head into the city, and the subways were not coping with it.

By the time I finally got on board a train, I had only twenty-five minutes to spare before the meeting started. No time to get a drink, no time to eat breakfast, no time to do anything but take my seat and pray that no one called on me. As I walked out of the train station and across the road to Bryant Park, the day's suffering started a few minutes early, in the form of torrential rain. New York City gets roughly twelve inches more rain a year than the United States' average. Our summers are crazy humid because it rains so frequently. All of this I knew well, and I could count on one hand the number of times I have left home without an umbrella. Sadly, this day was on that list.

I walked quickly up the stairs, toward the library entrance, shaking off my arms and legs like wet dog. I desperately tried to get my drenched hair off my face. Not only would I have to sit through hours of painstaking self-reflection, I would have to do so completely soaked.

I was just a few minutes late, but immediately Andrea greeted me with open arms and a disconcertingly wide smile.

"Lilly … we were beginning to think you wouldn't be joining us. Please sit," Andrea insisted. "Grant will be our lucky first to share his story today."

Apologising for my lateness, I took the last remaining seat, the exact same one I had taken the day before. Looking around the room, I noticed that everyone else was in the same seat they had been in the day before too. It's funny how that happens. It's like a little part of our physiology is stuck in elementary school with those God-awful seating plans. We take a spot, we get comfortable and we stick with it. Maybe it has something to do with the need to stay within our comfort zones or our need for routine.

The good news was that someone else would be talking today. I could sit back and listen, and now had more time to get things together before being called upon. The bad news was that I was still soaked and starving, and this moment, when someone named Grant was due to share the deepest and darkest parts of his life story, didn't seem like an appropriate time to excuse myself for a snack or to go to the bathroom to dry my clothes under a hand dryer.

"Whenever you're ready, Grant," Andrea said, gesturing to a man who sat directly opposite me.

I'd spotted Grant the day before, but I hadn't taken much notice of him. He was a middle-aged man, with an average build and dark hair. On the surface, there was nothing unique about him, but I guess that's how all the most incredible people seem – completely unremarkable, until you hear their story.

For what felt like a good hour but was probably closer to thirty seconds, we all sat in that dusty room, as the old air conditioner rattled along, waiting for Grant to speak. Finally, he took a deep breath.

"Hi … My name is Grant, Grant Hallisey," he began, shaking as the words left his mouth. "I am not entirely sure where to start."

"Start at the beginning, Grant. Tell us what happened that morning," Andrea said gently.

"Ok ... um … you know how they say that everyone has moments that make or break your entire life. Those moments that could go one way or another, the moments that if you had just done one little thing differently could have changed your life completely?" Grant questioned the room. "The stories of people narrowly avoiding the worst-case scenario were published everywhere in the wake of 9/11.

Limitations

They were meant to bring light to a dark situation, but they only ever seemed to make me more aware of just how easily life can change. I remember hearing about a guy who had worked every day of his adult life at the World Trade Center, but on the morning of September 11th his car had broken down, and in the time it took for a mechanic to make it to him in New York's peak-hour traffic, a plane had already collided with the north tower. But too often these stories went the other way, and our hearts broke for the intern on his first day in the big city who never made it back home." I join the rest of the room, nodding in silence.

"For me, that moment was as I stood at gate four of Newark Airport as Flight 93, destined for San Francisco, left the gate. I was meant to be on board, seat 1D. I would have been one of the first to die when the cockpit slammed into that abandoned field, but destiny had other plans. Things changed that morning, even if it felt the same as every other morning. Mary, my now wife but girlfriend at the time, had gotten out of bed a good hour before me. Her alarm roared beside me at 4am, one hour and forty-five minutes before we had to hop in a cab to make our way to Newark Airport. I had shoved her arm as the sound got louder, an attempt to pull her into consciousness. Despite packing everything the day before, she still felt the need to be up at that ungodly time of the morning." Grant spoke eloquently, but there was a shake in his words – like it hurt for them to leave his mouth. I made sure to keep my eyes on him in case he looked up, silently letting him know that I, a complete stranger, was there to support him. I knew it would help me if I were in his shoes.

"Eventually," he said, "my poking and prodding got too much, and she rolled out of bed, squashing the dog's tail under her foot as she stood up. As our border collie yelped and licked his injury, I grunted and placed my pillow over my own face, blocking out the light and noise Mary was creating. There was no need for me to be up that early. I had showered the night before. I was packed and ready to go. All I had to do when my alarm went off, one whole hour later, was get dressed and feed the dog. Mary didn't have to do too much more, but somehow, our 5:45am departure from the house was pushed back to 6:30am."

As Grant spoke about his girlfriend, I couldn't help but laugh to myself. Never have I related so well to a woman I had never even met – always up early, always trying to be prepared but as was reflected in my appearance on that day, always falling just short.

"I love my wife more that life itself," Grant continued, "but that morning I could have killed her multiple times. I did consider leaving her to suffer in economy on a later flight while I sat comfortably in the business class seats that my frequent flyer points had paid for. Instead, I responded to every one of her ridiculous suggestions with just a hint of sarcasm. When we finally left the house, New York morning traffic was in full swing and our street had transformed into a carpark. It took twenty minutes to get a cab, and once we did, it was another full hour before we arrived at the airport, which was so close you could smell the jet fuel."

For the first time since he started speaking, Grant averted his gaze from his lap to the room around him. His eyes were glassy and his bottom lip shook ever so slightly as he breathed in. How did it feel to have the eyes of an entire room directly on him? What was it like to share his heart and soul with a room of complete strangers? Grant gulped and returned his gaze back to the wedding ring on his left hand.

"For anyone that's following," he resumed. "We arrived at the airport at 7:50am for an 8:42am flight. At the end of summer. A smart man would have walked away or gotten a different flight, but we raced out of the cab and into the busy departure hall. This was long before digital check-ins, so there wasn't much hope of speeding up this process, but that didn't stop us from sweet-talking every staff

Limitations

member we could with a different sob-story. With only one minute to our departure time, and after hearing our names paged about twenty times, we finally made it through security. We ran with our small carry-on suitcases dragging behind us, and arrived at Gate A17 just in time. And when I say just in time, I mean just in time to watch our plane leave the gate without us on board."

I let out a little laugh, then promptly stifled it.

Grant looked up at me and smiled for the first time since he had started speaking. It was a tiny smile, subtle enough that in a blink you could easily have missed it, but it was there nonetheless.

"It's ok to laugh. It was pretty funny, looking back on it." He spoke directly to me, his tear-stained face softening slightly.

I smiled.

"I was so mad at Mary that morning," said Grant. "No matter how many times she apologised, how much effort she put in to book us on another flight and how happy she was that she got us on one that was just two hours later, I just wouldn't listen to reason. I had booked the entire trip. It was meant to be perfect, and from where I sat at that moment, she had ruined everything." Grant seemed to struggle with these words.

"I was on the way to the bathroom when I heard another page. It was nothing out of the ordinary until I heard 'All flights out of New York have been cancelled, effective immediately'. On the massive TV screens in front of me were images I could never have imagined: The World Trade Center, and our city, on fire. I stopped dead in my tracks, frozen, in utter disbelief, as we all were, I suppose. My heart broke and my mind raced. As I walked back to our gate, I heard screams and cries. People raced to payphones, every part of them shaking as they waited and prayed for an answer."

Limitations

I let out a tiny gasp. I often struggle to imagine what it must have been like in New York on that day, and as a rule, I do my best not to think about it. I was so young – so far away from it all. I saw things in black and white, dangerous and safe. I never thought about those on the ground.

"Just behind the lounge where Mary sat, I saw another large TV," said Grant. "The news blared, but Mary remained oblivious, engrossed in her book. I wondered if she had even heard the first announcement. Something in me wanted to go to her, to sit down beside her and pretend I hadn't seen what I had just seen. I wanted to keep her innocence intact for as long as I possibly could, but I couldn't lie to her about something so big. So, instead, I stood back and watched her for a while. The headline at the bottom of the screen now read, "America Under Attack" and underneath that, in small writing, "Flight 93 from Newark Airport Hijacked". My world shattered in an instant – that was our plane." Grant exhaled sharply as the words left his mouth, and ever so slightly, his body began to shake.

"Without a second thought, I ran forward, wrapping my arms around Mary and scaring the hell out of her. I explained what had happened and we sat there together in tears, in complete shock. We both nearly didn't live to see how the world changed after September 11th, 2001, and we both live every day very aware of just how lucky we are to be alive. But I haven't been the same person since that day. Along with a whole mess of other mental health issues, I haven't been able to step foot in an airport, let alone an airplane. I know how much Mary wants to travel again, like we used to, how much the kids want to go on holidays with me there too, but I can't do it. It kills me every day to watch her suffer because of the way I am, but I don't know how to change things for her. I have exhausted all known options, even hypnotherapy, and none of them have worked. So, that's why I'm here, to give my wife and children the life they deserve, not a life with someone who is too afraid to live."

Grant exhaled again, but this time, his once-rigid posture softened, and he gave into the pressure that seemed to be weighing down on his shoulders. His tears started to well in his eyes, and the room remained silent for what felt like a lifetime. All eyes were on Grant until … as if controlled by some exterior force … I stood up. I raised my hands in front of my body and clapped them together once, twice, three times, and over and over again until the rest of the room joined in. The strength it must have taken for Grant to sit in front of all of us, sharing the most troubled parts of his soul, to be the first in the group to do so and to not run and hide – it's one of the most commendable things I have ever witnessed.

My heart broke for him, but on another level, I was inspired and honoured to have been in the room to hear this story. I have honestly never been so proud of a total stranger

in my entire life.

Chapter 5

By the time we finished, I was starving and freezing cold from my morning drenching. I had spent our short break desperately trying to dry myself off in the bathroom and had no time to grab anything off the snack table before we started again. I hadn't gotten far with the drying process either, for that matter.

The second they let us go, I was up, bag in hand, ready to escape. I rushed down the stairs and out of the library's front door. I didn't stop for a second to look back until I reached bottom of the front stairs and heard the soft but sturdy voice of a man behind me.

"Lilly, right?" the voice asked.

I whipped my head around at the sound of it. I was startled by the familiar face in front of me. He was young, probably not much older than me, and attractive, but I couldn't put my finger on where I knew him from.

"Do I know you?" I asked politely with a half-smile.

He smiled back at me – the kind of perfect smile that makes you forget all your problems while, somehow, simultaneously creating more.

"That was really amazing what you did today," he replied. Everything clicked, and I realised that I was face-to-face with one of the members of the group who I had noticed the day before – the boy so certain that it reflected across every inch of his face. And today was no different. He looked so determined – like he had a goal in his head and there was nothing that could possibly stop him from achieving it.

Limitations

"First seat to the left, right by the door?" I replied,
pointing at him.

"Ah, the master detective has worked it out. I prefer
to go by Harry, but whatever works for you." He laughed.

If I am being honest, there was something about him
that kind of made my heart stop. The way he looked at me –
it was like I was some interesting new discovery that he had
an innate need to investigate. His eyes were the brightest
blue I had ever seen, his skin seemed to glow in the
afternoon sun. And I looked like a drowned rat whose
stomach wouldn't stop growling from hunger … typical.

"Hi, Harry. And thank you. It was nothing though.
That guy was so brave, speaking first. He deserved it," I
replied, smiling and fiddling with my hair in a futile attempt
to make it more presentable.

"You got caught in that downpour this morning,
hey?" Harry asked, laughing gently at me.

Embarrassed, I stopped fiddling with my hair and looked up at him with an awkward smile.

"Don't even get me started. The one day I don't pack an umbrella. And I haven't eaten since last night ... I'm a mess today." Stop oversharing! "And you don't care about that, so I'm going to stop rambling now and go catch my train." My sentence trailed off as I pointed toward the subway and started to walk away, mortified with my constant ability to embarrass myself.

For the record, this was precisely why I was so closed off to romantic ventures. Men made me nervous; they always have. If they were even remotely attractive, they may as well have been a totally different species because I certainly couldn't communicate with them. I haven't had the best luck with men in the past, so a year or two back, I gave up trying, settling into a life of solitude … at least for a little while. I learnt that it all hurts too much when it inevitably falls apart, so it's easier to never start. I was a hopelessly damaged mess.

"Lilly," he called as I started to walk away. "I haven't eaten since breakfast; did you want to grab a late lunch? I would love to hear about how much of a mess you are," he laughed as he spoke, pointing toward the café that sat on the edge of Bryant Park.

"Uhhhh," I murmured hesitantly, looking down at my phone searching for some reason to run as far away as possible.

I looked up at him, his smile was wide and eyes shining in the summer afternoon sun. He was incredibly attractive, not that that matters, but it certainly wasn't going to be hard to spend a meal in his presence. I exhaled, reluctantly giving in to his offer.

"I really should eat," I stammered.

"There we go," he joked, beckoning me to walk with him.

*

We sat at the furthest table from the café, the only one left. At that time of the afternoon, the park was filled with students, tourists and workers all taking breaks from their own busy schedules. I ordered a salad and water, trying to look like one of those girls who can survive on that kind of rabbit food, and he ordered a sandwich and a green tea. We talked for what felt like hours.

It turns out he was a year older than me, a second-year medical student at NYU and was insanely knowledgeable about things I had never given a second thought. He knew the dates that structures were built and remembered train timetables without having to check his phone every five seconds. In fact, in the time we spent together, I don't think I saw him touch his phone once. He seemed wise beyond his years. It was kind of intimidating if

Limitations

I'm being honest. We spoke about everything, from our favourite TV shows, to tastes in music. It was effortless – it felt like we were meant to be there in that moment, talking like we had nowhere else to be.

I told him where I had come from originally, and he told me he had moved to the city with his family from Los Angeles when he was quite young too. We bonded over how hard moving was in general and how, when you're that young, New York City seems to swallow you whole. He told me how he desperately wanted to see Australia, and everywhere really, and read off a big list of all the places he had been to so far. I told him that as much as I wanted to, I had never really travelled anywhere other than Australia and America, and this seemed to shock him.

After speaking for just a couple of hours, it felt like we had this insane bond that I had never experienced with anyone else I had met before. It wasn't awkward or uncomfortable. It was the kind of connection you have when you're a kid, when you meet that other weird kid who just gets you perfectly – you spend every second together before one of you plays with the wrong person and the whole thing implodes in the most dramatic fashion.

I waited for it to all blow up or to wake up from this crazy dream, but it didn't happen.

In all the weird and wonderful topics we covered, one thing that never came up was why either of us were in the therapy group. For the life of me, I couldn't see any sign that he needed any help at all. He seemed to have it all figured out, and I couldn't even remember to eat breakfast and pack an umbrella before I left the house. I wanted to ask, but I knew that would mean opening myself up to being asked the same question, and I just wasn't ready for that. So, instead, we opted to ignore the elephant in the room – or the park, more appropriately.

Chapter 6

The sun was still bright in the afternoon sky, but it was getting late. I had so much I needed to do at home, but I had no desire to leave, so I did all I could to keep the conversation going – not that it was hard with him. I couldn't help but laugh internally at the anhedonia diagnosis I had received a few years previous. I had always thought it was ridiculous, I was never incapable of feeling pleasure, I just didn't always believe that I deserved it. But if I had any reservations that that diagnosis had been complete and utter bullshit, they all disappeared in Harry's presence.

"So, what do you do with yourself outside of college and the support group from hell?" I asked.

"Mostly, I work at the Brooklyn Museum. I love it there," he replied with a smile, his pride evident.

"Oh no … " I answered, not even thinking before the words left my mouth.

Harry stopped for a second and then laughed, as if he knew what I was talking about.

"I know, I know, I'm a bit of a nerd," he replied, laughing.

"Oh, no, I respect that – I can get on board with that. I was 'oh no-ing' the Brooklyn part. Don't tell me you're one of those deconstructed coffee–drinking Brooklyn hipsters?" I replied, placing a hand to my face to feign shock.

Harry laughed at my terrible acting and raised his hands in fake surrender.

Limitations

"I'm actually much more of a tea drinker," said Harry. "And you will be pleased to know that I drink it every morning on this side of the East River. I love Brooklyn. I just hate the vast majority of the people who live there." He smiled.

"Oh, thank goodness. I will never get on board with the lame Brooklyn hipster trends, and it's our generation that starts them all ... it's embarrassing," I laughed, shaking my head in disgust.

Harry paused for a second. His eyes locked on me as if realising something for the first time, and he smiled, laughing ever so slightly.

"If you ask me, there are only two good things that have come out of Brooklyn: the museum and *Brooklyn Nine-Nine*," Harry replied, counting the two things on his fingers.

"I have never agreed with anything more ... Well, the *Nine-Nine* thing anyway. I will admit I've never been to the museum, but I'll take your word for it." I laughed awkwardly.

"Wait, what? Are you serious? You've never been to the Brooklyn Museum? Oh my god, Lilly, you have not lived. It's one of the best in the city." Harry stretched his arms out as if he had the power to show me the whole city in one look, and for a second, I believed him.

"Hey, give me a break. It would take me like an hour on the train and would seriously cut into my reading hours," I replied, before realising how lazy that made me sound. "I really should go though. I always found ancient history really interesting. It amazes me that thousands of years after a story was first told, little pieces of it are left behind for us to put together, like a puzzle constructed by history." I blushed with a nervous smile.

Harry appeared to be shocked by the words that had come out of my mouth. He never stopped smiling, and it seemed impossible that anything I said could make him happy.

"Well, on that note, you have to come with me. We could go now!" Harry shouted excitedly, grabbing his backpack from under the table and placing it on his lap ready to go.

Shocked, I stared straight at him, and then at my phone to double-check I was reading the time right.

"Now! It's like 4pm. By the time we got on a train and got there, it would be closed, wouldn't it?" I asked.

Harry laughed. "It would definitely be closed because it doesn't open today, but nothing is impossible. You can get in anywhere if you try hard enough. Or if you have an access-all-areas pass for special staff members," he said with a devilish grin.

"Are you seriously suggesting we break into the museum where you work? After hours? Couldn't we just go after the meeting tomorrow or something?" I placed my hand on the table in front of me as if trying to ground his insanity.

"I mean, we could," said Harry, "but what would be the fun in that? Come on, it's so much more magical at night without tourists crowding every exhibit. I guarantee you will love it." The excitement in his eyes was adorable.

It was just occurring to me that I had literally just met this guy and had no idea who he really was or what he wanted from me. Though it was becoming clear that he was completely and certifiably insane.

"What if we get found out?" I said. "Because I am fairly certain that's how this story would end."

I had enough going on in my head without an arrest piling on top.

"The guards in that place are more incompetent than Hitchcock and Scully. All we have to do is be quiet and they won't suspect a thing. And ... if for some reason they do, you can play the innocent bystander card – you had no idea I wasn't allowed in there after hours. I swear, I'll take the blame." Harry placed his right hand to his heart and raised his left to the side of his head.

"Very funny." I laughed, certain that this was all some big joke that would stop soon.

"I'm being dead serious ... Come with me," Harry said sternly.

I didn't want to give in, but, oh my god, when he looked at me like that, it was all I could do not to catch on fire.

"I literally just met you. Why on Earth should I trust you?" I asked, laughing nervously.

"Oh, come on, if I was going to murder you, I would do it without subjecting myself to the 'support group from hell'. I would corner you with my piercing blue eyes – you know, the ones you haven't been able to look into since we met." Harry winked, causing a redness to spread across my cheeks.

He wasn't wrong – I had avoided looking into his eyes at all costs. If I did, I would just get nervous and turn into the same awkward mess I usually was. With him, in this moment, I felt like one of those girls who could meet and interact with a guy without embarrassing themselves or having to pretend that they were anything they weren't – I had certainly never been that girl before.

"You think you're smooth, but you're really not." I shook my head at him.

"Just trust me." He stood up, looking down at me, as if everything hung on what choice I made next.

I took a deep breath, weighing up the choice in my head.

Cons:

-       You hardly know this guy; he could be a serial killer for all you know.

-       There is a very real possibility you could be arrested.

Limitations

- You might actually turn to stone if you look into his eyes.

- You are not in any way prepared for your session tomorrow.

Pros:

- He's very attractive and super-sweet.

- You are always saying you want to live more.

- You weren't going to get any prep done tonight anyway.

Fully aware that the cons outweighed the pros, I stood up, grabbing my things from under the table, and looked him up and down cautiously.

"Don't make me regret this," I whispered.

As we strolled together, the air seemed to get warmer. I don't know if it was just the heat on a New York summer evening or a reaction to the person who walked beside me ... But I didn't hate it.

By the time we got off the train, it was nearing 5pm. Brooklyn was abuzz with peak-hour traffic, and we walked against the grain towards the museum. About 150 metres away from the main entrance, Harry grabbed my hand, pulling me away from the main street and down a side street. The contact and the sudden jolt made my heart stop.

"Still not murdering you, I promise," he whispered coyly. "It's just easier if we go in through the staff entrance. Less cameras."

"I have read enough books and watched enough TV shows to know that 'I'm not murdering you' is almost definitely something a murderer would say. You know that, right?" I laughed hesitantly.

Harry stopped in his tracks just outside the staff entrance and looked me dead in the eyes. "I am aware of that." His tone and expression gave me chills.

Limitations

Then he broke his gaze and laughed.

I stood frozen.

"Scared you, right?" he laughed before stepping forward.

"Don't play with me like that, man." I gave him a fake death stare, which was met with another cheeky smile and wink.

I watched from behind as Harry pulled out his staff ID card and scanned his way into the building.

"Won't they know it was you who scanned in?" I asked.

"They could find out, but they never check that. And if they do, I'll just say I left my keys here or something. I'm a trusted employee. Just relax," he replied softly.

"Yeah … I can see they have good reason to trust you," I replied, rolling my eyes.

"Hey, don't think I spend every day breaking into museums with different girls I pull off the street. I swear

I've never done this before." Harry laughed and I laughed too, wanting to believe him but falling just short.

The inside of the museum was a stark contrast to the outside world. It was dark and icy cold, like stepping into a closed refrigerator. Harry grabbed my hand in the darkness, causing me to jump. He turned his phone light on to help us see and directed me toward an exhibit marked "The Wonders of Ancient Egypt" in bold white writing.

We wandered through the halls, hand in hand. I had to keep telling myself that this was so he could guide the way and nothing more or else I might have gone into cardiac arrest. We stopped for a few moments to look at each exhibit before moving on. Right near a mini recreation of the Great Pyramids, my foot accidentally knocked a trash can, and the loud bang echoed throughout the room. We both stopped in unison, staring at each other. Then Harry swiftly pulled me away into a nearby corner. He placed his hand over my mouth to keep me quiet, and we stood there for a few minutes, silent and out of sight. No one came to check if there was an intruder in the exhibit. There was no other noise but the sound of us breathing. These guards really were incompetent.

"I think we are safe," Harry whispered after a few minutes.

"That wasn't terrifying at all." I laughed, as we stepped out of the corner and into the open space.

"Next time," said Harry, "try stepping away from the trash can, not stepping into it."

"Excuse me, I can't see a goddamn thing. You are my eyes. I take no responsibility." I raised my hands on either side of my face in surrender.

"Come on, you. This next part is really cool." Harry grabbed my hand once more.

We walked past the pyramid and through massive black double doors. The next room was a large, wide-open space. It was better lit than the last room, allowing Harry to turn off his phone light. On the floor, there were at least fifty squares, about six square feet each. They looked like they were made from some type of black tape. The ground was illuminated by a purple light.

Harry looked at me, let go of my hand and sat inside one of the black squares.

"Don't look up – just sit down with me," he whispered.

Shaking at the smoothness of his tone, I did as he said and watched him as I sat down on the floor.

"Are you ready for this?" he questioned, not taking his eyes off me for a second.

"I'm genuinely starting to think you are going to murder me, but sure, we've come this far – why not?" I laughed.

I couldn't take my eyes off him and he didn't take his off me. My heart beat faster than I ever knew was possible.

Limitations

"Look up," he whispered.

So I did. On the roof was one of the most beautiful displays I have ever seen. Stars, millions of them. In New York City, you don't often see stars – there's too much light – they are always drowned out. But inside this room, we could have been miles away from New York City, in a time before any other light source was known.

"It's a representation of the night sky on the approximate date that the Great Pyramids were finished in Egypt. Brighter than we will ever see it again," Harry explained as he looked up with me.

"This is amazing! I have never seen anything so beautiful." I could feel his gaze on me, but I remained focused, mesmerised by the roof above our heads.

"I could say something really cheesy right now, but I won't," he whispered.

I pulled my eyes away from the roof and looked him deep in the eyes. My heart beat rapidly and my breath hitched in my throat. "Say it …" I began. "Shoot for the stars – they're closer than they seem." I nodded to the roof above us.

Harry just stared into my eyes for what felt like a lifetime, before finally leaning in. He kissed me softly, gently, like he was asking for permission. It caught me off guard, but once I settled into it, nothing ever felt so right. I pulled away after a few seconds, giggling to myself awkwardly.

We sat there for a few minutes. Not saying anything, just looking up at the fake stars. We were just about to kiss again when ...

A voice bellowed from the next room. "Is someone in there?"

My heart stopped, frozen with fear. Harry, however, jumped into action. In one swift movement, he jumped up, grabbed my hand, and pulled me to my feet. Then, together, we started to run.

Limitations

"We have to move quickly," he whispered. "There's an emergency exit just over here. It used to have an alarm, but it's been broken for a while now."

With heavy breaths, we ran side by side, past different exhibits and toward the illuminated, green exit sign.

When we got outside, we didn't stop – we just kept running, the New York summer-night air rushing past us. After a few blocks, I stopped, releasing my grip from his hand and struggling to catch my breath.

"You are completely insane, man! We could have been arrested!"

"I knew what I was doing – we were totally safe," he replied with a fake laugh.

I just laughed as I desperately tried to catch my breath.

"It was amazing though, right?" he asked.

I wasn't sure what part he was talking about – the pyramids, the fake night sky, the kiss, the running for our lives or that we found each other today – but my answer was the same either way: "Once-in-a-lifetime level stuff."

Limitations

Dear Lilly,

No, no, no, nope, hell no!!! If you go down this path, if you let him in like you want to, it will end in tears. He will break your heart. He will leave like everyone else, and you're not strong enough to handle that. Or he might die! What if you fall in love with him and he dies?

I'll admit, he is kind. He sees the world differently to anyone else I have ever met. He doesn't seem like the kind of guy that would break your heart. Also, a side note, he is an incredible kisser.

Group isn't going as badly as you had expected. The people are inspiring – they delve into the deepest parts of themselves and actually find something worth talking about. You can learn a lot from them...

From Lilly

Chapter 7

Why?! Why did I break into a museum with some weird –
but admittedly very nice – guy I'd only just met? Why did I
let him kiss me? And why the hell did I like it so much? It
has been a long time since I kissed a guy and even longer
since I enjoyed it.

I have never been a hopeless romantic. I'm all for
supporting fictional relationships, but real world
relationships just end in tears. And should this really have
been my priority? For the first time, I was trying to be
committed to a journey to improve my mental health, and

there I was, lying in my bed thinking about some stupid guy's lips on mine.

A news alert popped up on my phone's screen, illuminating a Facebook notification from 11:49pm last night – "Harry Crawford sent you a friend request." It was as if the universe was playing some cruel trick on me!

I opened the notification and clicked on Harry's profile. There was a photo of him beside a statue of Sherlock Holmes, geotagged in London, United Kingdom. I smiled foolishly at his cheeky grin. But it was Harry's cover photo that surprised me most – a photo of Harry, much younger than he was now, with four other boys. They stood together in front of a massive lake with bright blue water, and vibrant trees lining the waterfront. The photo was captioned with a quote from Mary Shelley's *Frankenstein*, one of my all-time favourite books – I was a little impressed. I closed the photo and clicked back to my notifications. Hovering my finger over the accept and decline button, I contemplated whether I

Limitations

would regret accepting the request in a few months' time when Harry had, inevitably, cheated on me. But despite my anxiety, I caved and accepted the request. My phone started buzzing in my hand. It was the second alarm and my cue to get up as quickly as possible.

*

When I arrived at the library, I walked inside immediately, hoping to avoid seeing Harry and any awkward small talk. The person he met the day before was not me. I don't know what the hell got into me, but he would not meet the same person today. It all seemed like a story, a fantasy. Part of me wanted to forget it all, but no matter how hard I tried I just couldn't help replaying it like a movie in my head and smiling to myself like a goddamn fool. That was, until I walked into the therapy room and saw him sitting there. He smiled at me – that same damn smile. And just as quickly as it had happened yesterday, I was back in the alternate universe where this all seemed like a good idea.

I smiled back shyly and took my usual seat.

A few short moments later, Andrea plodded in, completing the circle of "survivors" – at least that's what she said as she sat down.

"Ok, day three. Let's get today started," she commenced, looking down at the list of names in her hand. "Dwayne Greer?" she asked, looking into the circle of people.

I let go of the breath that I didn't know I'd been holding on to. I'd been so caught up in everything, I didn't even think about the very real possibility that she may call on me. Looking around the circle, I saw a man raise his hand. It was the firefighter I had noticed on the first day. He seemed more wary today.

Andrea nodded to Dwayne.

He took a deep breath.

Limitations

"When I woke up that morning, something felt different," said Dwayne. "There was something in the air that took me back to my childhood, to a happier time. You know when you smell something in the breeze? It might remind you of the schoolyard or a childhood breakfast. I think that's the feeling you get right before everything changes. I think it's the universe giving you one last little breath of the good times, of the happy memories, before things change so drastically that you won't be able to remember these insignificant details anymore. Because, from every moment after that, you will pray that you could go back to that simpler time."

Dwayne was sure of himself. You could tell he had been thinking about this moment for a long time. Thinking about the moment where everything good and right in the world was taken away in an instant.

"I didn't know two planes were going to crash into the World Trade Center just a short few hours later – but something felt off balance. I took a deep breath as I exited

my apartment block that morning, grabbed a cup of coffee

from the bodega just outside my home, walked through the

narrow passageway to get to the parking station and drove to

work. When I got to the station, it felt the same as always.

The strange feeling had dissipated, leaving behind the stench

of routine. Everyone spoke the same way they always had:

my friends, co-workers, even my boss, made jokes. Usually,

when we got the call, we didn't think twice – another routine

building fire. In most cases, it was an alarm system that had

been triggered automatically. But they told us it was "high

priority", so we sprang into action, prepared for the worst

but expecting much less. No amount of preparation or

training could have prepared us for the reality. We drove as

quickly as we could. As we got closer, things started to blur,

the world wouldn't focus. Inside the fire truck, we could

hear the screams, through the air conditioning vents, through

the tiniest cracks in the windows. We heard the screams and

then we saw the smoke. We were about halfway there when we realised that something horrible had happened. This wasn't an overcooked bagel. It wasn't a fork in the microwave. It was something much bigger."

Dwayne stopped, blinking more in a minute than what I think a normal person would do in a week. It's a common physical symptom of PTSD – you see it on television all the time.

Dwayne flinched as Harry gently placed his hand on his shoulder.

"Hey, man, it's ok if you need to take a break," Harry consoled.

It took Dwayne a moment to slow his breathing. Finally, he turned to look at Harry and smiled, ever so slightly.

"No, I'm ok ..." Dwayne replied taking a deep breath. "Thank you," he said, nodding to Harry.

Harry nodded back, removing his hand from Dwayne's shoulder. I was suddenly filled with admiration. I tried desperately to stifle the smile that was threatening to spread across my face.

Dwayne composed himself. "There were curse words thrown everywhere as we jumped out of the truck," he said. "By the time we got there, the World Trade Center was a mess of smoke and flames. We ran in, only thinking about the people on the inside. I can't remember much about being inside that building, not chronologically anyway. It all blurs into one big mess. I can, however, still see ash burning innocent people's faces, and dismembered body parts falling from the sky. I won't easily forget the shrieks – the last moments of people's lives, ripped away from them in a pit of fire and smoke and toxic fumes."

I felt a shiver go down my spine, causing every hair on my arms to stand on end. I tried not to think too often about those poor people inside the tower, nor how horrible their last moments must have been. It's amazing how complacent you can be when you are so far away. How self-centred you can become, focussing on your own fears and emotions alone.

"I realised, in that moment, that we would be solidified among the worst parts of human history. New York City, the shining star on America's Christmas tree, fell to the ground, crashing into thousands of tiny pieces at the base of the World Trade Center. The rest of the tree followed suit. I often wonder how long it took the people on the planes to work out that they weren't going to make it home. I wonder if they begged and pleaded for their lives or if they just sat there, admiring Manhattan's beautiful skyline until they realised how close they were. I hope that that's how it went anyway. I hope that none of them suffered like the people in the buildings. I hope it was so quick that they didn't even have the chance to think about all the life they wouldn't have the chance to live."

My heart broke as I heard Dwayne say those words. All his pain was based on empathy – he felt for those who could no longer feel for themselves. I had seen him on day one and assumed he was a big tough firefighter who was burned in the line of duty and was scared about it happening again, but I couldn't have been more wrong.

"In the days that followed," said Dwayne, "I couldn't really function. As soon as we declared that the search was over and that anyone else who was meant to be there was gone, I broke. For days, I had been so strong. I had held it together because that's what we needed to do to get those few people out safe. It was that, and only that, that kept me together, that kept me sane. I lost friends – people I'd trained with, worked with, and people I'd spent most of my adult life with were gone just like that. My best friend was one of them ... he didn't die. Though, honestly, most of us wish he had. He's been in a mental institution ever since, on constant suicide watch. He'd rather leave this life than live in a world where planes just fly into buildings and there's nothing we can do to save the people inside. That's why I am here, because part of me feels like I should be where he is now. Instead, I just sit here, an unrecognisable shell of the man I used to be. What no one tells you about being a firefighter is how many people you can't save. What happened that day, no one asked for it, no god foretold it or instructed it to happen. But it did happen, and when it did, it was my job to help the people impacted, and I couldn't do it."

Dwayne looked down, but it seemed like he had more to say.

"You know it wasn't your fault, right?" I assured him. "There is only one party to blame for that day. You are the hero of this story, not the one at fault."

"That's sweet of you, but it's just not true," said Dwayne. "I left my job shortly after that day. I couldn't forgive myself enough to jump back in again. I couldn't lie to another desperate human, telling them that everything would be ok when I knew full well it wouldn't be. I work in security now, for an ATM collection company. I can never go back and change what happened that day, but I'm here so I can learn to live with myself and attempt to get back to doing the only thing I ever wanted to do with my life, without the constant guilt and memories of that day hanging over me."

As Dwayne finished speaking, the room sat in silence until the sound of a chair squeaking broke it. It was Grant. He stood, just as I had yesterday. He looked around at the circle, beckoning them to stand with him. We all rose, clapping together. I could see tears forming in Dwayne's eyes as the applause settled down and people returned to their seats. I stayed standing.

"You are an incredible human being. For just a second, even if you can't be proud of what you did that day, be proud that you had the strength to speak about it with us

today," I declared before returning to my seat.

"Thank you," Dwayne said under his breath, a tear

falling from his eye and down his cheek.

Chapter 8

Andrea was characteristically unhelpful for the remainder of the day's session. In her defence, I really do think she was trying, but for someone in her position, she seemed to be rather unfamiliar with the concept of survivor's guilt.

"But you saved so many?" she implored.

"But so many more died," Dwayne replied, his voice shaking with each word.

"Is that your fault, Dwayne?" Andrea asked.

"Not first-hand ... but is it fairer that they died and I survived?" Dwayne asked defensively.

Limitations

I saw the pain in his eyes. I felt it in the way his voice shook. I saw how much he desperately wanted the questioning to stop, if only for a few minutes. Did I handle what happened next the best way? Probably not. But in that moment, did I feel it was necessary? Absolutely.

I vividly remember a moment in fifth grade when Maria, one of my best friends at the time, went through a particularly messy "breakup". After a public screaming match on the playground, she ran to our compulsory music class with tears streaming down her face. She sat with her head down on the desk, crying so loudly that it drowned out the class's tinny recorder renditions of "Hot Cross Buns". Listening to her cry broke my heart. I wanted nothing more than to pull her out of that room and away from all the stares. So, I did exactly that. While everyone else split up into groups, we escaped through the front door of the demountable and hid under the metal stairs, chatting and laughing until the end of class. Unfortunately, we were busted on the way back into the classroom to retrieve our bags and found ourselves in what would be my first and last lunchtime detention. I have strong morals – I pride myself on doing the right thing, but when I see someone hurting, all those ideals go out the window and this innate need to help takes over. This need is what found me replacing our names on the detention list with the name of our teacher just to see my severely wounded friend smile once again. This might have been the first time that I found myself in this position but it would certainly not be the last.

We had just a ten-minute break in a five-hour day – hardly enough time to go to the bathroom let alone get anything to eat. Most of us just sat in the room, making small talk and eating what we could off the small snack table. So, when Andrea signalled the break, I jumped straight up, dodging Harry who had been trying to grab my attention from the other side of the circle. I ran down the hallway toward the bathroom.

Limitations

I opened the bathroom door, checked to make sure no one was in the stalls, and reached up to the red box above the hand dryer – the fire alarm. I took a deep breath and pulled down on its handle. Nothing happened at first, but I remembered reading somewhere that there is often a couple of seconds delay with these things, so I quickly ran out of the bathroom and back to the therapy room just as the alarm began to ring out.

By the time I entered the room, everyone was in full-blown panic mode.

"What the hell is going on?" asked Harry who seemed to be looking directly at me.

I had to give it to Andrea – in a room full of manic psychological cases, she stayed completely composed. Her hair was ruffled and her glasses were askew, presumably from the shock of hearing the alarm go off.

"Fire alarms have been activated," said Andrea calmly. "We need to leave the building. Everyone head to

Exit C, and we will reconvene there." She pointed to an emergency exit map on the wall, then grabbed her notes, straightened her glasses and walked past me through the open door.

I didn't want to say anything that might incriminate myself, so I just shrugged at Harry and muttered, "I guess there's a fire." I quickly grabbed my bag off the floor and walked out of the room ahead of him, hoping that he couldn't see the ever-growing smile on my face.

The fire department was already there by the time we arrived at the meeting point in the park near the library. The sirens drained out the ringing of the fire alarms and had managed to attract a swarm of onlookers. Dwayne looked shell-shocked. Admittedly, setting off a fire alarm may not have been the best way to get an ex-firefighter with a serious case of PTSD to relax, but in that moment, it was the absolute best that I could come up with.

Limitations

It didn't take long for the firefighters to declare that it was a false alarm and allow the library to reopen for the remainder of the day. By this point, however, it was nearing 1:30pm and Andrea, whose glasses were once again uneven and hair was reminiscent of Albert Einstein, had clearly had enough.

"Well ... that was enough chaos for one day," said Andrea. "I think we can call it a day. I will see you all tomorrow." She shuffled off away from the group and toward the library's entrance.

I watched as Dwayne exhaled, his look of relief growing. He strode over to the group of firefighters who were packing up their equipment nearby. He greeted them, and they all cheered and laughed together. His entire body lightened around them, like the weight of the day was lifted. He seemed to be more himself than he had been inside that room. I would hazard a guess that he was acting more like himself than he had been in twenty years. It couldn't have been more obvious that he was where he was meant to be.

They say there's no such thing as a selfless good deed, and maybe that's true because, watching Dwayne, I couldn't help but smile.

"So, are you avoiding me?" Harry said behind me, making me jump out of my own thoughts and, literally, jump on the spot. I turned around to see his smiling face, his bright eyes.

"If I wanted to avoid you, you would never see me again." I waved my hands in front of my face like a magician. "It's just been a weird day, I guess," I finished, suddenly feeling stupid.

"It has been indeed," he responded. "So, why'd you set off the alarm?

"What?" I snapped, in a way that no innocent person ever would. I had intended to play the role of the innocent until proven guilty – girl who was simply in the wrong place at the wrong time. That was until he smiled at me – it was a soft but devilish smile, which made me feel, almost, like he was proud of what he believed I'd done. I don't know why I was surprised. The guy was obviously some crazy delinquent who got off on chaos, but still, you don't expect support when you act on one of the craziest decisions of your life – it threw me off guard.

"How did you know?" I replied.

Harry smiled again and shook his head at me slightly.

"You were not gone for long enough to pee, and you came back into the room like five seconds after the alarm went off ... oh, and you have red paint flakes on your shoes from the fire alarm." Harry pointed at my shoes and folded his hands behind his back like a smug investigator.

I wanted to be mad at him for how closely he watched me, but honestly, I was kind of impressed.

"You know what? That is impressive. And you call me the master detective." I laughed.

"Thank you very much," Harry responded with an over-exaggerated bow before adding that his examination may have been inspired by a love for crime shows. "So ... why?" he asked.

"Dwayne looked like he was about to have a full-blown mental breakdown in there, Andrea wasn't helping, and I couldn't watch it anymore. I'd seen the alarm a few days back. So, I thought I'd give it a shot," I explained as if it wasn't a completely ridiculous decision.

Harry smiled again, wider this time, and nodded his head.

"Well, I'm impressed – not only is that super-sweet, but it's also 'break-into-a-museum level crazy', and I respect that." He winked at me.

I shrugged, trying desperately to suppress the redness that threatened to spread across my face.

Limitations

"I learnt from the best," I replied.

Harry laughed an awkward laugh that faded quickly and then looked around, as if he was searching for the right words to say.

"Did you want to go get some lunch or something?" he asked awkwardly.

I didn't want to let him down, and part of me really did want to have lunch with him and end up on another crazy adventure, but I needed to be alone. I felt a darkness spreading inside of me that threatened to take control if I didn't just escape it all for a few moments.

"I really wish I could, but I can't," I said. "Today has been weird, and I need to get home and do some things ... I'm sorry."

Harry looked defeated as the words left my mouth.

I didn't know where this journey of self-discovery would lead me, but if I knew one thing, it was that this was something I needed to do alone. It was how I worked best –

away from the pressure to be someone or something I was not, and just be solely me.

"Right ... that's ok," he said softly.

You know when you tell a puppy they will have a walk and no walk is delivered, they look at you like their whole world has ended? That was the exact look on Harry's face.

"Maybe tomorrow?" I said, trying to bring his usual beautiful smile back to his face.

Harry gave me a small smile and nodded. "Yeah, tomorrow," he whispered.

Chapter 9

I was not one to hide from distraction. That is to say that if a happy thought threatened to take over the darkness that was filling my mind, I would never shut out the happiness. In fact, I go looking for it: I find books and television shows and music that distracts me in my darkest moments; I make compilations and playlists; and when it all gets too much, I fade away into the light of someone else's life. But up until that moment I had never found the light in the eyes of another person. I had never felt warmth and peace in simply thinking about them. I had never had something real to drain out the darkness, and now that I did, I was terrified to let it in for too long. I was terrified that, if I let him in – if I let him consume my thoughts –the darkness would overcome me and nothing would be bright enough to drown it out when, inevitably, he was taken away. So, I shut my mind off and chose to focus on the darkness, allowing it to take me wherever it wanted to.

I had every intention of heading home, but in an instant, I changed my mind. I ran up the stairs of the train station and over to the other side to head downtown. I jumped on the first train that came, stood up the whole way and got off at Wall Street Station.

At this time in the afternoon, things were relatively quiet up that part of town. Most people were still at work, so it was just tourists that flooded the streets, of which there were plenty. But still, I had seen it a lot busier than that. I strode briskly up the stairs from the train station and up through Wall Street. I followed the narrow pathway all the way to the end and turned left, and that's when I saw it: The

Limitations

One World Trade Center, a glistening shrine casting a shadow over the already forsaken place. Something about it always haunted me. It was meant to show our strength, but all it did was remind me of the awful thing that happened there. Something about the singular building, so different to the ones that came before, reminded me "they" had won.

I sat down on a wooden bench near the memorial for the old World Trade Center. The afternoon sun reflected off the skyscrapers that surrounded me, blinding me as it bounced into my eyes. My eyes closed, protecting themselves. I had been to the memorial hundreds of times, but for some reason I thought it would be different today. Maybe I had been inspired, or maybe I just wanted an excuse to escape Harry's interrogation, but this afternoon this place just spoke to me. It was as if the fallen had called to me across New York City, "Come sit with us, Lilly."

Nope – I cringed – that's creepy.

Aimee J Edwards

I pulled out my small black moleskin notebook and a green sparkly gel pen from my bag. I always carried these with me, in case inspiration struck or to remind myself of something important. Mostly, it was filled with random ideas I had had on the train, and had abandoned before I arrived at my destination, along with quotes I had read or clever titles for books that I would never write. This time, I turned to a brand-new page and wrote a singular word title "Why?" Then, underneath I wrote a list of things that were bugging me, thoughts and questions I couldn't get out of my head.

- Why New York City?

- Smoke? How much?

- Why that day? Was the emergency call number (911) relevant to the chosen date?

- What about the fact that the number 11 looks like the old World Trade Center?

- Did the victims know they were going to die?

Limitations

- How many people got out of the buildings?

- Did they get a chance to say goodbye?

- Were there any dogs inside?

- How did anyone who saw it first-hand continue

  to breathe?

- Why do things like this happen?

- Why can't I just be happy?

- Why did it impact me so badly?

- What could I have done differently?

- Why was I not worth fighting for?

- When did I give up, just like he did?

If I'm being honest, none of it really provided any perspective. But having written the words on paper, having let them out of their cage, I didn't feel quite so consumed by their presence.

I continued to scribble incoherent notes in my notebook before a voice behind me made me jump for the second time that day.

"Writing the next New York Times Best Seller?" he asked.

When I turned around, I was face-to-face with the same person I had just left behind at the library.

See, this kind of thing creeped me out, and was the precise reason I was single. I didn't ask him to follow me. For that matter, I didn't even tell him where I was going, and yet here he was like some superhero trying to save the day. I didn't want to be saved. All he was doing by being there was scaring the hell out of me.

"Sorry ... I didn't mean to scare you." He laughed, almost as if reading my mind.

"Harry!" I started. "What ... the ... hell? Did you follow me here?"

Limitations

"Um ... yes ... and evidently, I did not think about how creepy that would seem," he replied, bowing his head slightly.

I said nothing. I just looked at him, my distain persistent and unwavering. I tell you if looks could kill he would not have made it past that day.

Harry jumped into defence mode, but unlike anyone I had ever met, he remained utterly calm the whole time, with not even the slightest hint of anger.

"I have read enough books to know," said Harry, "that when the flight risk from your support group – who you happened to kiss the day before – runs away, you should definitely follow her." A redness spread across his cheeks.

"Harry!" I yelled. "This isn't *The Fault in Our Stars*! We are not going to run away to Amsterdam, fall madly in love and return for your untimely death a few months later!" I paused for a moment, trying desperately to regain my composure. "You don't need to run after me. If I run off, it's because a. I have somewhere I need to be, or b. I'm going somewhere to be alone. It's not your job to solve whatever is going on in my head."

Harry looked shocked but he nodded.

"Um ... firstly ... spoiler alert,' he said, "that book has been on my 'to be read' list for months."

I laughed, shaking my head at his inability to be serious for longer than a few moments.

"Secondly," said Harry. "I'm sorry ... I was just worried about you. You seemed a little jumpy."

I exhaled and rolled my eyes. He was like a persistent puppy dog who desperately wanted a pat. He had nothing but good intentions, and Cruella Deville over here could do nothing but yell at him. God, I should definitely stop comparing him to a puppy dog.

"I'm a fairly jumpy person. You might want to get used to that." I laughed, gesturing to the seat next to me.

Limitations

Harry nodded and took the seat beside me. "Noted," he whispered. "So, what were you working on? If it's ok to ask?"

"Eh ... nothing major." I sighed looking down at the now closed notebook. "I guess I'm just trying to work it all out – what brought me here, why I'm such a mental case and all that fun stuff," I said with a fake laugh.

"You don't know?" he responded sharply.

It's a completely logical question when I think about it now, but it seemed kind of ridiculous at the time. Does anyone know? Does anyone have any idea what is happening to them? Aren't we all just walking around waiting for something to make sense and then, when it does, moving on to the next puzzling life question?

"I don't know anything ... my life sometimes feels like a story with missing pieces that was placed inside my head by someone else. None of it feels real, but then, all of a sudden, it's so real that I can't breathe, and it continues like that on an endless cycle."

The water splashed below the memorial fountain, creating a supernatural haze on the surface that gave me the chills. My heart beat rapidly in my chest. It seemed to speed up with every thought. All I could do was take a minute to breathe and bring it back down to normal.

"My dad died here," Harry stated, cold and unmoving. "I was six ... I couldn't explain it or understand it. When Mum told me he wouldn't be coming home, I laughed and said 'Cool, does that mean we can have breakfast for dinner like we always do when Dad is away?' It took me years to really work out what happened. I was so young – it was easy to push the memory so far away that it began to feel like someone else's life," Harry finished.

I gently moved my hand to rest on top of Harry's. "I'm so sorry ... I had no idea," I whispered.

Limitations

"Of course you didn't. I didn't tell you, and I would be really creeped out if you did know." He laughed before shuffling his hand to grip mine. "The point is," he said, "we all feel a little lost sometimes. Like the life we are living is not our own, like we are just voyeurs watching from a distance. The important thing to remember is that that feeling is perfectly normal." His thumb brushed circles on the back of my hand. "Pain is just another reminder that we are alive – just don't allow it to drain the life out of you." He smiled subtly.

I gazed deep into his bright blue eyes. "You're too wise for your own good. You know that, right?"

"I am quite aware of the depths of my intelligence, yes," he responded, feigning immodesty. He jumped up from the bench as if it might kill him to focus on the dark thoughts for longer than a few minutes. Maybe it would. Maybe that's why he was constantly making jokes and was seemingly full of endless energy.

"So, what are we doing this fine afternoon?" asked Harry. "I hope you don't say 'staring into the distance until we both slip into madness', but if I'm with you, I suppose I could get used to it." Harry laughed, jogging on the spot in front of me like he couldn't contain his energy.

As much as I desperately wanted to hide from all my problems, I knew I couldn't do that forever. He was a bright and shiny distraction that I could certainly get used to having around, but that's not what I needed today.

"Not today, man ... I think you are right. It's time I stopped letting the pain take my life away. It's time I find some answers," I replied, smiling up at him.

"How exactly do you intend to do that?" he responded, slowing his jogging down to a stop.

"I haven't the slightest clue ... but I'm going to find out," I replied, standing up and flinging my bag over my shoulder. "And I will see you tomorrow in group." I finished with a smile that I meant more than any of the fake ones I had given that day.

Harry looked me up and down with a cheeky smirk. "You promise not to ignore me next time?"

"I'm not in the business of making promises I can't keep, dear Harold. You will have to wait and see." I laughed, placing a small kiss on his cheek, and walked slowly toward the subway station.

I can't be sure what Harry did after that. Though something about him made me think he stood frozen in stasis until the next morning when he teleported to the group meeting – like he was some robot, invented for a purpose that I was not yet sure of. But he made me feel safe, comfortable. He seemed to care what was going on with me, even when I didn't, and the peace that came along with that was refreshing.

When I arrived at the train station, the previous train had just left. I sat down on a nearby seat and opened the notebook again. Under the very last point, I added one more:

  o How can I tell if this is too good to be true?

Limitations

Dear Lilly,

He's kind. He cares. I have done nothing but push him away all day and he still followed you all the way to the memorial. Is that creepy? I still can't decide.

I can't go down this path. When it ends, which it will, I will break. Am I strong enough to pick up the pieces?

But he is broken too. He has been through so much worse, and he somehow manages to stay positive and optimistic, not just for himself but for other people, people he barely even knows. I wonder what he's hiding behind all that hope.

Maybe he's right – maybe it's time I stop letting fear and pain get in my way.

I don't know what comes next, but at least I finally have some decent notes to work with.

From Lilly

Chapter 10

Fear is uncontrollable. It takes hold of you in your weakest moments and is omnipresent even in your strongest. Its overwhelming power is enough to reduce even the bravest human to tears. And then, just when you think you have overcome it, it comes barrelling back in like a runaway train, knocking you completely off guard. Professionals will have you believe that the way to overcome fear is to face it head on, but I would argue that logic is severely flawed. If, like me, you fear losing someone you love, how are you supposed to face that? Are you expected to kill someone? For as long as I can remember, my two biggest fears have been elevators and planes. So I guess, deep down, my fear is falling with no way to save myself. Read into that what you will, but something in Harry's bright blue eyes scared me in the same way.

On the way home, I browsed the internet for reasons that survivors return to the "scene of the crime". The results were remarkably uninspiring. Of them, a thoroughly depressing *Washington Post* article that contained a video of survivors of mass shootings returning to the scene of the crime, a Yahoo! Answers question about what Survivor contestants are allowed to bring, and an incredibly dull looking book about survivors returning to work. I didn't find too many answers to my own problems, but I can tell you that Survivor contestants do get a complete package of essential items including tampons and birth control.

The next two days of sessions went by in the same way as the ones before, minus false (fire) alarms, of course. On Friday, we heard from a young girl, India, who was born

Limitations

a few days after the attacks on the World Trade Center and never got a chance to meet her father. India told us that her mum never got over losing her soulmate and cried herself to sleep for months on end. She felt that her mum should the one in the support group. India's story broke Harry – I could see it in his face as she spoke.

*

After India's session, I took Harry for lunch at a café up the road from the library. It was one of my favourites, and I knew it would make him feel better. He wasn't acting like the same person I had come to know over the last few days – he seemed withdrawn, like the world was spinning around him faster than he could comprehend. I knew he'd been hiding something behind his strong exterior, but now that I saw it, I didn't know how to help.

"You have to try this cheesecake, man. I guarantee it will be the best dessert you've ever had," I promised as we walked through Bryant Park.

"Sounds good," he mumbled softly.

As we sat down, I sighed, looking at his broken, helpless face.

"I wish I could help – the way you do," I whispered.

"What do you mean?" he asked.

"You always know exactly what to say – you have the perfect pep talk. I can see you're hurting, and I want to help, but I don't know how." I reached to grab his hand but then pulled back slightly, second-guessing myself.

Harry looked at me and smiled for the first time since India began talking. He reached forward, grabbing my hesitant hand in his own.

"You're here ... that's enough," he whispered. "And I'm ok," he continued, his voice breaking slightly. He shrugged and shook his upper body as if there was a bug on his shoulder. "It's just that hearing stories like that … they bring up some of the worst thoughts from my past." He shrugged.

"Remember, all feelings are valid." I raised my arms like Andrea, mimicking her hippy nonsensical wisdom that provided no assistance to humans who were struggling.

Harry laughed at my joke, his smile brightening up the dimly lit café.

"So, I believe that cheesecake was promised?" he asked, raising an eyebrow at me, and with that, I called the waiter over and ordered two strawberry cheesecakes. And as promised, they were incredible.

*

That weekend, we met at the same café, walked around the city, petting as many dogs as we could find, and taking silly tourist photos in front of monuments that we had seen almost every day of our lives. In Times Square, Harry stood with his arms outstretched and back arched, like all the tourists who tried to capture the glory of Broadway in one single photo. At the Statue of Liberty, I posed with one hand on my hip and the other stretched to the sky with a street hotdog in hand. In Central Park, we took silly selfies with the city and the water in the background. I listened as he spoke highly of friends whose names I can't remember. I didn't know who any of them were, but I felt I owed each of them a debt of gratitude for playing any part in shaping the person I was coming to know.

As the sun began to set on Sunday evening, we hired a rowboat and sat in the middle of the lake, watching the sun set over the city that never sleeps. Harry took photos of me on his phone when I wasn't paying attention, and when I was, I poked my tongue out at him, ruining all his pictures, but he saved them anyway.

Limitations

On our way back to the shore, Harry stopped rowing. Behind me, he grabbed my oar. I was startled by the sudden stop, and the boat rocked beneath us.

"Oh, my god ... you scared the hell out of me." I laughed, stabilising myself before regaining control of my oar and using it to splash water in his face.

Harry wiped the water off his face and smiled at me, but his expression quickly turned serious.

"Hey," he whispered, looking at me intently.

"Um ... hi?" I questioned sarcastically.

"So, we can't keep doing this. You know that, right?" he said, as if he had had a completely different afternoon to me. Because from where I sat, I could easily spend every day of the rest of my life sitting here with him, escaping reality.

"I know, we need to get the boats back in the next few minutes," I said. "What are you talking about?"

"At some point, you are going to need to tell me why you are doing this?" he replied.

"Doing what?" I asked, brushing my hair away as it blew into my face.

"Therapy! The support group from hell, I believe you called it?" He laughed. "What happened, Lilly?" he finished, looking at me seriously. His eyes seemed to penetrate my soul.

My heart dropped into my stomach as the words left his mouth. For the past week, I had been caught in a delusion, one where I could be level-headed and somewhat normal. I had allowed myself to get wrapped up, to be that girl who meets a guy and doesn't overthink it – well, not too much anyway. But I had forgotten somehow that we'd met in a support group, and of course he had questions. He had delved into his past with me and I had remained silent, but that couldn't happen anymore. The elephant in the room had

Limitations

jumped into our boat and if we didn't talk about it – we would sink.

"I was five when it all happened. But I still remember it like it happened yesterday. I went downstairs to watch the morning cartoons, but someone had switched the channel since the night before. It was everywhere," I said, desperate to get the words out before the weight of them pulled me under. "I felt like I couldn't breathe when I saw it. For years I was scared of my own shadow and now ... I feel like I'm constantly waiting for the worst-case scenario to come around and drag me under."

Harry watched me intently, like he was lingering on every word I said, trying to take it all in.

"I need you to understand," I said, "that the reason I don't talk about this isn't because I'm closed off or because I'm too scared to open up. I genuinely don't know why it impacted me so badly or why it still does. I just know that I haven't been the same since. My dad left the same day – a problem child was never really his style, and I'm not sure he ever really loved me or my mum that much anyway. I've only seen him once since, and I have no desire to see him again," I said, looking past Harry and at the city lighting up in the distance.

"You don't think seeing him might help?" he asked.

I knew it wouldn't. If there was one thing in my life that I was sure of, it was that no good could ever come from seeing that man ever again. Harry would give anything to see his dad again, but his situation and mine were very different – his dad didn't choose to leave him, his dad didn't decide that he wasn't worthy of a father's love and affection – mine did. He believed that seeing his father would solve all his problems.

I couldn't break him by telling him he was wrong. So, instead, I just shook my head.

"I know it doesn't make sense," I said. "I don't know how else to explain it. Honestly, Harry, I wish I did. I

just know that I am not alright, and I'm holding myself back.
I know I need to fix that if I ever want a life." I gazed at his
face and fought the urge to breakdown on the floor of the
boat.

"I'm sorry, I didn't mean to upset you," he
apologised softly.

"I know you didn't. It's ok. I'm ok," I whispered. "I
just wish I could explain it to you. I know it's not easy to be
around me when I'm so closed off to a whole part of my
life."

I waited for him to agree – for him to quickly row us
back to the shore so he could run away as fast as possible –
but instead, Harry rolled his eyes.

"You are quite honestly the easiest person to be
around, no matter how closed off you may be from time to
time. When you are ready, I will be by your side, ok? If you
need anything at all, any help or just someone to stand

beside if the world feels like its crumbling around you, I'm here," he replied, looking me deep in the eyes.

You know that feeling when someone says exactly what you want to hear and you are caught between kissing them and pushing them into the Central Park Lake? Ok, admittedly, that is probably specific to this situation, but that is exactly how I felt.

"Come on, weirdo, don't get all sappy on me. We need to get this boat back to shore." I laughed, picking up my oar and splashing him once again.

*

As I walked home later that evening, the moon shining high in the sky above me, I realised that my biggest fear wasn't dying in a plane crash or falling to my death in a broken elevator, it was watching Harry walk away and not learning how it felt to fall in love with him.

Chapter 11

The world is a scary place. We can't go to a concert without scoping the venue for an easy exit strategy should something go wrong. Children can't safely go to school without fear of losing their lives to a lunatic with a gun bought from the nearest Target. Most people spend every single day in fear of their life for some reason or another, and we're expected to just keep going. There are times when it feels like every single miniscule force in the universe is working against me and my happiness, and it's all I can do not to curl up in a ball and just cry. The reality is, the world isn't a safe place, good people are hard to come by, and all you can do is distract yourself from all the darkness – find the brightness in the little things – before it consumes you.

When my alarm went off the next morning, I didn't growl or complain. I didn't wish I could throw it to the other side of the room and curl back up to sleep. For once, I was happy to be getting up. I sat up, rubbed my eyes and checked my messages. Six notifications from various news outlets, two likes of a sunset pic I posted to Instagram late last night, twelve spam emails and a Facebook message from Harry that said, *Thanks for one of the best weekends I've had in a long time. I hope I didn't overstep with all the questioning.*

I smiled for a few minutes at the message. Harry has this way of back tracking when he says something serious – like he's afraid I will get the wrong idea and everything will fall apart. I've never met another person who is so innately good and so determined to make sure no one ever thinks of him in any other way. But he's not self-centred – he's not just another guy wanting to make sure that everyone likes him. It's almost as if it would genuinely hurt him if anyone

thought for even a second that he had a bad bone in his

body.

Eventually, I got up, got dressed and left the house

with enough time to get breakfast. I still didn't have the

faintest idea what I was going to say if I was called upon,

but for some weird reason, I didn't mind. I stopped at the

same coffee shop Harry and I had eaten lunch at the week

before and ordered a banana and blueberry smoothie and a

green tea. As I waited in the park, a Dalmatian puppy

fetched a stick, bringing it back to its owner over and over

again. His owner kept his face in his phone the whole time,

only looking up to pick the stick up and throw it again. He

was missing the joy on his puppy's face and the way the

little dog's ears flapped up and down as he ran along the soft

grass. We so frequently distract ourselves from all the pain

in the world. I wonder how often we miss something so

beautiful when doing so.

*

Harry smiled widely as I walked in the therapy room and handed him the green tea I had purchased. I headed toward my seat before stopping suddenly. I stared at the seat I had been sitting in every day for the last week – it looked cold and uninviting – like someone had claimed it over the weekend and I was no longer welcome.

"I'm sure Dwayne wouldn't mind switching," Harry said gently. He smiled at me once more, even wider this time.

"Don't think this means anything," I said as I sheepishly took the empty seat beside him.

"I would never be so inconsiderate as to read into anything you do, Lilly." He laughed, poking his tongue out at me.

The remainder of the session was a rollercoaster of emotions. Aaliyah, a Middle Eastern woman, probably in her early forties, spoke about her loss of faith in the wake of the attacks. Harry and I ate donuts during the break, laughing at the sugar it left on our faces. By the end of the session, I was emotionally exhausted and I just couldn't get Aaliyah's words out of my head. "September 12th, 2001 was the last day I wore a hijab. My connection to my family, friends and my faith was ripped from my head, figuratively, and literally by the bigot who decided I had personally orchestrated the attack on New York."

These words spun around my head and left a mark on my heart.

Aaliyah was afraid to share her religion with the closest people in her life. I can't imagine how painful that must be. The strength she must have, to raise her children to live differently to the only way she's ever known. I wanted to tell Aaliyah that it would be ok, but I didn't know how. Twenty years on and xenophobia was still such a prevailing notion in our country, and it had only been reignited by the man in charge over the last four years. How do you tell someone that everything will be ok, when you aren't sure you believe it yourself?

"Sometimes I feel selfish?" I said to Harry as we walked out of the library.

"Selfish for what?" he asked.

"For daring to feel hurt after something like 9/11 when there are people who have gone through so much worse."

"I'm a pretty firm believer that everyone has the right to feel whatever emotions they happen to feel at any given moment," Harry whispered firmly.

"But Aaliyah had to throw away her entire life, all her morals, her entire belief system because of something she wasn't even directly involved in. I mean, sure, you have every right to not be ok. But me?" I asked, my voice unsteady. "What ever happened to me? What right do I have to feel this way when someone went through something like that?”

"Lilly, you do know that you're allowed to not be ok, right?” Harry asked.

I shrugged and kept walking, my mind a swirling mess of emotions. The truth is, I didn't know that. There was something else that came along with the constant fear and anxiety that plagued my mind, and that was self-doubt. I didn't just doubt that I was good enough or capable enough. I also doubted that I had any right to feel this broken when everyone I met had more of a reason to be broken than I did.

As if reading my mind, Harry took hold of my hand and led me through the park to a massive fountain.

"Do you know about this fountain?” Harry asked, like a school teacher questioning his class.

"I do,” I replied, unsure where this was going. "It's the Josephine Shaw Lowell Fountain. She was the first woman in New York City to be honoured with a monument.

She founded The National Consumers League that advocated for consumers on market and workplace issues," I said, basically regurgitating the information from my old textbook.

"Good memory," he replied. "Did you know that she lost her husband in the Civil War only a year after they were married. And then, one month later, she gave birth to a daughter, Carlotta. All of this was long before she did anything that you mentioned. She found herself in the depths of despair and she built herself back up."

I stared straight at him, listening intently to every word he said.

"It was hard to be a human after 9/11, Lilly. Even if you didn't directly lose someone in those towers ... How are we meant to get up and go on like nothing happened after something like that?" he replied solemnly. "Life might go on after the world stops, but it's never quite the same," he finished with such purpose in his voice that it gave me chills.

Limitations

"How is it that you are so smart?" I asked, taking hold of his hand in my own.

"Remembering things like this just helps me come back down to earth when the world feels like it's going to spiral out of control." Harry rubbed the back of his head. "It's weirdly comforting to know that people have been through worse things than me and that they were able to get back up and move on. It gives me hope." Ever so gently, Harry rubbed circles on the back of my hand.

I understood him more in that moment than I had before. All his little pep talks – they were as much for him as they were for me. His wisdom, the light he tried to put into every single conversation, that was his coping mechanism, just as writing, books and television were my own. He needed to present an image of a person who had it all together or he would lose control.

"You know you don't need to do that around me, right?" I asked.

"What do you mean?" he replied, looking at me quizzically.

"You don't need to present that front that you always put up. You're allowed to break if you need to. I won't think less of you for it," I whispered, tightening my grip on his hand.

Harry looked intently at me, his face softening.

"I know, but I'm ok. I swear," he whispered back.

"Ok ... but just remember that for future reference," I replied, and sensing he didn't want to talk about it, I quickly changed the subject.

"Did you want to go on an adventure?" I asked as we walked past the fountain and further into the park.

"Always," he replied with a smile and a wink.

With a smile and a wink back at him I grabbed his hand and strode, as fast as I could and with as much purpose as I could muster, through Bryant Park. In all the years I had lived in New York City in our small apartment, there had been one other thing that had always managed to pull me out

of my own head and back down to earth. I had never spoken

about it with anyone but my mother, but right now I wanted

to share it with Harry.

Chapter 12

The room was dark and musty; the only light came from a small weak lightbulb that hung from a single cord in the centre of the room. The walls were lined with boxes, stacked upon shelves, each filled with piles of paper and a thick layer of dust.

"I take you on a nice peaceful private museum tour and you bring me to a dirty closet ... I think it's obvious who's winning the dating game." Harry laughed, looking around him.

Dating? I felt my face turn red.

Limitations

"Peaceful museum tour?!" I laughed. "This is a win for me. You just don't see it yet." "Ok ... so what the hell are we doing here?" Harry said.

"This, my friend, is the biggest collection of untold stories you will ever find." I waved my arms as if to present the room to him.

Harry looked at me like I was speaking another language, and then, with one eyebrow raised and a puzzled tone in his voice, he asked, "Untold stories?"

"When I say untold stories, I mean unpublished books – more than you could ever possibly imagine. One Christmas morning, our toaster blew up – it was quite dramatic. Our entire family was sitting around the table, and the bacon and eggs were ready, but the toast was not going to happen. So, Mum sent me down here to look for an old toaster, which was stored in a box a few years back, and instead, I stumbled upon this room," I explained. "I imagine someone who worked for a publisher lived in the building and didn't want to throw the unwanted manuscripts away, so they kept them down here, and when they moved, they weren't able to take them with them. I've googled, though, and every single one ceases to exist on the internet. Every single one has been read by probably two people, tops, and left down here, lost to time," I finished, my hands brushing over the dusty boxes as I spoke.

"I have to say, when you said we were going back to your place," said Harry, "this isn't exactly what I had in mind."

For a second, my heart stopped.

"But – I will admit – this is pretty damn cool," he replied, pulling out a box and taking a look inside.

"Of course, it's cool, man! Would I bring you anywhere uncool?" I said. "I like to sit here and read, and imagine what these people did with their lives after they were rejected from publication. Because the thing is ... they are all amazing. There isn't a book down here that I wouldn't recommend to anyone I met. These are tiny little pieces of someone's soul and they've been left here and forgotten."

I riffled through a box and found a thick stack of papers with the title, *A Puppet on Your String* by Marie Andrews. "Here," I whispered, taking out the first page of the manuscript and handing it to Harry. "Read this aloud." I moved to the corner of the room, dusted the floor to remove any cobwebs and sat down to listen.

Harry looked down at the piece of paper in his hand and took a deep breath. "Like a flower, caught in the hands of time, I freeze, waiting for you to return," Harry read softly. "My heart breaks for you, and yet you leave me here, alone, abandoned, destined to be nothing more than just your puppet on a string." He looked up to me.

"Keep going," I said, anticipating what I already knew would come next.

"I wasn't yours to use, but you chose to use me anyway. I wasn't yours to change, but I will never be the same. In your wake, you left nothing but fragmented flowers, squashed into the ground, forgotten and unrecognisable," he finished, his face fell.

"Brutal, right?" I asked with a soft giggle.

"It's incredible. Who is this woman?" said Harry. "How did anyone reject something so beautifully written?" He turned the page over as if he was looking for evidence to prove me wrong.

I stood up, taking the piece of paper from his hand and returning it carefully to the pile.

"Everyone has a story," I said, "but the world is a money-making machine. Not all stories are going to be told. It hurts me to think how many never will be."

"That is incredibly insightful," he replied with a small smile.

"Never underestimate me, Harold." I winked.

Limitations

"So where do you think the author is now?" he asked. "Wouldn't it be amazing if we could find her, let her know how incredible her story is or at least let her know that someone read it?" he asked excitedly.

"Sadly, I know the answer to that question." I stared down at the stack of papers. "It was one of the first ones I read. I looked her up and she died only a few years after she finished the manuscript. She never had the chance to know that someone would feel the way we just did hearing her words aloud. It was after I found that out that I decided not to look up the authors – imagining the lives they might've led after these manuscripts were finished was much nicer than the reality of untold stories."

"So, what would you imagine for her?" Harry moved closer to me and brushed a stray hair out of my face.

The feeling of him that close made my heart jump, but I composed myself.

"I imagine that she is somewhere beautiful, where she can sit and read and look at a field of fresh wild flowers every day. A place where the sun shines in her window every morning, waking her up at the exact right moment. And I picture her slowly, but surely, rebuilding herself – hopefully with someone who sees her, like, really sees her for who she really is, not just as a puppet that's there to do what someone else wants of her." I found myself whispering.

Harry was even closer to me by then. His hand was placed ever so slightly around my back, holding me in place and holding me up. I looked deep into his bright blue eyes, and the world around me melted until he was the only thing I could see.

"I see you," he whispered before leaning in and kissing me deeply on the lips.

I pulled slightly out of the kiss, swallowing and looking him deep in the eyes once more. Then I leaned back

Limitations

in and kissed him with everything I had inside of me. Harry wrapped both arms around my back and lifted me up into the air. And then, as if I had been doing so my entire life, I wrapped by legs around his body and kissed him intensely. Harry moaned slightly and pulled his lips away from mine. His smile was intoxicating. He pushed me up against the storage room door and kissed my neck.

The two of us connected like we had been made to fit together. Our souls intertwined as our bodies did. Nothing felt as good or as right as the two of us did together in that moment.

Chapter 13

I was eighteen when I first, well ... did the thing Harry and I just did. It was in the backseat of a beat-up old Ford truck, and it was disappointing to say the least. Mostly because we were eighteen and hiding in a car, but also because I didn't believe it was meant to feel exactly right unless you were with exactly the right person. It was two years and some heartbreak later that I tried with a different person. It didn't feel right when he had my consent, and it certainly didn't feel right when he didn't. Not a single person – not the serious relationships or the one-night-stands in nightclub bathrooms – ever felt right. But with Harry, there was no awkwardness or fear of doing the wrong thing. We connected, and it was just right.

I don't remember falling asleep with Harry, but I know I was the first to wake up. As the light bulb on the roof flickered, Harry draped his arm over my shoulder. I rolled over, burying my face into his chest as he began to stir. Harry groaned slightly.

"It's a crazy time of the day to be sleeping, Lilly," said Harry in a voice that was deeper than usual. He cleared his throat and whispered softly, "Hey, wake up."

"There's a lot of crazy going on today." I laughed, raising my head up to look into his eyes, and placing a gentle kiss on his soft lips.

Sitting up on the dusty floor, I found my clothes in the corner and began restoring my body to its prior form. I laughed to myself – as if any part of me would ever be the same after that.

"I'm not sure putting those back on is completely necessary," Harry joked with a cheeky smirk.

"You'll get over it." I laughed, winking at him and flicking his bare chest with my shirt.

After re-dressing, I took Harry upstairs to my apartment, and we sat together for a few hours, talking, cuddling and watching afternoon television like nothing had just happened. In his arms, I didn't feel so broken. It felt like his strength was holding me together, and though it flew in the face of everything I believed in, it felt right in that moment.

"Uh, you should go," I snapped after our third episode of *Say Yes to the Dress* had finished with a massive fight and the entire bridal party leaving the store.

"Wow, rude! Most people send a hint, but you are just straight to the point, aren't you?" He laughed, sitting up on the couch.

Limitations

I shuffled on the couch to face him. "I'm sorry, I would love for you to stay here, I swear. But ... my mother will be home soon, and I just can't deal with that right now. This is super fun, and I like you, believe me, but it's new, and I don't need any more questions from her than I already get."

"No, it's fine ... I understand," he whimpered, his voice cracking into a fake sob.

"Get out, you loser." I laughed, pushing his chest playfully.

Harry wrapped his arms around my back and pulled me in for a kiss. Then he got up and walked toward the front door.

"Until we meet again, Lilly," he said with an exaggerated bow before opening the door.

"Bye, Harry," I responded sweetly. He walked out and closed the door behind him, leaving the world spinning around me.

I lay on the couch and stared at the ceiling for what felt like forever, smiling like a little kid and thinking about our time together. The television kept playing trashy lifestyle shows in the background, but I was too distracted to take any of it in. It was my phone that finally pulled me out of my daze. It buzzed once, and then again. Still lying down, I pulled it out of my pocket and brought the screen up to my face. There were two texts:

One from Harry: *Don't want to be creepy or anything, but I miss you already : '(*

And one from my best friend Ella: *Hey, Girly :D You free for dinner tonight?*

Ella and I had been friends since grade school. She was now in her final weeks of post-graduate study, and for her, finding a minute to send a text was like finding a needle in a haystack, let alone finding a night off. This was the girl who had celebrated with me when I got my first period. She was my biggest supporter. I shared everything with her, telling her things before I even admitted them to myself. It

suddenly occurred to me that she didn't know about Harry or

the support group I was going to. Yes, absolutely, I would

make myself free for dinner.

I opened my texts and replied, *Careful, Harold, you

wouldn't want to seem too keen :P*

And, *Absolutely! 7pm @ TGIFS? :D*

*

At TGI Fridays, I sat in a booth waiting for Ella to arrive.

She walked in, blonde hair a tangled mess and her handbag

draped awkwardly over her shoulder. Ella was effortlessly

pretty; she always had been. In any situation with Ella, no

matter how good I looked or how smart I was, I was always

the ugly dumb friend. But it didn't matter. She never made

me feel less. For as long as I can remember, Ella had been

building me up, and during our darkest times, we had leaned

on each other like a crutch. She was just a few weeks out from sitting the bar exams and was about to start a fascinating career, but here she was, the same as always – my person – the Christina Yang to my Meredith Grey.

Ella and I ordered the potato tasting extravaganza – a dish of our own creation that consisted of mashed potato, cheesy bacon potato skins, fries, tater tots and whatever else we could find that had potato in it. We had begun this tradition in the throes of a rather dramatic breakup – I couldn't remember if it was mine or hers – but it had become the foundation for our girl's night ever since.

Under the fading spotlight that hung above our booth, I told Ella about everything from the last week: the support group, explicit details about every single conversation, and about Harry.

"Ooooh Harry – hot name!" Ella began. "So, looks-wise, are we talking more Styles or Potter?" she questioned with a wink.

Limitations

"Styles all the way, but he's also smart, like super-smart. He is as smart as Harry Potter looks like he should be." I laughed, pulling out my phone to show her one of our many photos.

"Ooooh, girl, you hooked a live one." She laughed and mimed a fisherman pulling in his catch. "So where are we at? Have you reached the awkward "will they, won't they" kiss stage yet? I hate that stage!"

It was amazing how well Ella knew me. She knew exactly what I was like by analysing all my past experiences, but Harry was different. I think Harry and I were always meant to be – from the first hello, there didn't seem to be any doubt.

"Oh, we definitely did," I responded.

"Kiss?" she yelled. She looked around before promptly turning back to await my answer.

"I mean, there was kissing involved, I guess." I laughed, knowing that she would catch my hint.

"Oh, my god! Lilly, you dirty girl!" she yelled again, this time loud enough that a few people on nearby tables with children turned and glared in our direction.

"Oops." I laughed.

I raised my hands to them, silently apologising for her outburst. But, in typical Ella fashion, she did not give a damn who heard and who was offended by it.

"So, what was he like?" she asked, poking me in the arm.

"I am absolutely not going to tell you that." I laughed, shoving a potato skin in my mouth.

"Oh, come on! Do you realise how long it's been since I've had sex? I'm too busy to even deal with it myself these days! You gotta give me something!" she replied, practically on the edge of her seat.

"You are sick – you know that, right?" I laughed.

Ella laughed with anticipation in her eyes and continued to poke my arm.

Limitations

With a soft smile, I said the only words I had been thinking since that afternoon.

"It was ... perfect".

Dear Lilly,

Harry is hot. You slept together, and it was way way way more fun than it should have been. It never felt like that before. You've never felt this way before.

Margaritas are amazing! ... I forgot why I thought writing this was a good idea.

Good night, Lilly.

Chapter 14

That night I dreamt of running away to a long, white, sandy beach where waves crashed freely onto the shore. And for the first time, I didn't do it alone. I imagined living the rest of my life in an island paradise, reading and writing with Harry by my side.

When I woke in the middle of the night, I was scared, and I didn't even know why. Maybe it was the fear of letting my guard down or that I was not prepared in any way to be called on in the support group, or maybe it was just the margaritas from the night before. All I knew was that there was an ache in my stomach that no amount of Tylenol could settle.

The next morning, I woke up to my phone alarm buzzing on my chest and the sound of Ella snoring on my bedroom floor. I was still dressed in the same clothes as the night before.

"Ella," I shouted, shaking her slightly with my foot until she began to stir. "Why didn't you sleep in the bed, weirdo?".

"Hey, I don't know what you've done in that bed!" She laughed groggily, pulling herself to her feet.

*

Ella and I parted ways at the train station an hour later. She was off to college and I was off to the support group that was starting to feel like a full-time job. Every time Ella and I departed, it felt like the last day of high school all over again. She was so focussed and driven that it was sometimes months before we'd see one another again, but every time we did, it was just like old times.

She smiled at me and said, "Take care of your heart, baby girl," before heading to her platform. I don't remember where the quote came from. It might have a book or movie we were studying in English in the later years of high school, but ever since we heard it, it had stuck with us. It had become our mantra when one of us was going through something new or scary, and it always seemed to ground us. It was a reminder that it was ok to look after ourselves too.

*

"Dude ... what happened to you?" Harry asked with a laugh as I sat down next to him. My hair was half-done; I had no make-up on; and there were more bags under my eyes than in the overhead lockers of a 747.

"I had dinner with a friend, and dinner turned to into drinks ... and I regret everything," I replied, burying my throbbing head in my hands.

"Drinks? On a Monday night?" He laughed loudly. "Aren't you a wild child?"

"Could you kindly turn your volume down." I playfully pushing his face away.

As the last member of the group sat down, Andrea began her usual spiel that always ended with the name of that day's speaker.

"Harry, whenever you're ready." She nodded in his direction.

I knew why Harry was here, but if I am being completely honest, I didn't really know the half of it. He had become this beacon of light in all the darkness that hung around this room. I know it was selfish and horrible to think, but part of me didn't want to know how broken he really was – it was better that he remained the pillar of strength I had known him to be.

Unfortunately, I was incapable of stopping the inevitable. Harry took a deep breath to prepare himself.

"I'm Harry. I think we've covered that already, but whatever." He laughed as he spoke. I knew this trope – he would laugh, act strong, pretend like he wasn't hurting, when, deep down, it was killing him.

I nodded to let him know I was there and to encourage him to continue.

"I was six years old when the attacks happened on the World Trade Center. My dad worked on floor ninety-four of the first tower. He was one of the first to die. He didn't get a chance to think twice about whether to escape or stay put – he had a few seconds of what I can only imagine was sheer panic before he was killed on impact. I didn't understand it at the time, and, if I'm being honest, I probably still don't. I used to plead with my mum, asking questions like, "If I brush my teeth properly, will daddy come home?" I was so young, and I thought I'd done something wrong. I thought it was something I could fix by being a better son, but there was nothing I could've done. I wish I'd known that at the time because I still have nightmares about the pain in my mother's face as she answered those kinds of questions."

Harry was definite in the way he spoke, but when his voice broke, it sent chills through my entire body.

"For those who don't know, I'm a medical student at NYU. I start third year at the end of the summer. In second year, they do a skills lab training day. It's basically a simulation. They get a whole heap of dummies, come up with a huge accident that happened involving them all, and write out little cards for each patient with an overview of their involvement in the accident and their condition on arrival at the hospital. Our job was to act like trauma attendings, to make decisions about patient care and keep the patients alive and healthy. The patients were people who had been mowed down by a car in an outdoor shopping mall. My first patient was an innocent bystander, a woman in her late twenties who had been knocked headfirst into a pole by the car. She had several broken bones, but the most pressing injury was a subdural haematoma."

The entire room looked at him like first graders in a first-year college lecture. I laughed at their blank stares.

"That means a blood clot that forms between layers in the protective coverings of the brain," I explained, proud that I knew the answer.

Harry looked to the side, startled at my response.

"What?" I said. "I watch *Grey's Anatomy* – I know things." I laughed, and the rest of the room joined in with me.

"So," said Harry, "what the assessors were looking for was for us to get a neuro consult and ultimately decide to operate to neutralise the clot, and I did exactly that. I received an easy 100% for my first patient. My second patient was caught underneath the car when it went up in flames. There were burns to 90% of their body, and I was meant to begin with standard burn protocols, but I froze up. I forgot everything I had been trained to do. We needed to help every patient to pass, so I got my first fail grade. The patient was a 30-year-old male and a father of one, and I couldn't help but think about my own father. The reason I decided to pursue medicine was to help the helpless, like my dad. Instead, I stood there, frozen in my tracks and unable to remember anything I had learnt in the years prior. The patient succumbed to his injuries in the end. Some of my classmates said that with such severe burns that probably would have happened anyway, but I believe I could have saved him if I had have worked for it. I know he was just a dummy, but I can't help thinking about what happens when I graduate, when I start my intern year and have to deal with real patients with real burns and real families waiting for me to tell them that everything is going to be ok. I'm here because I'm scared that this thing in my past is holding me back. After all these years, I haven't dealt with it properly, and I don't want to live a life where people die in front of me through no fault of their own. I want to be the kind of doctor who saves the lives of the unfortunate and gives them a second chance to be with their families again. I often wonder how I might have been able to save my dad. I don't want to feel that helpless in another situation. I don't want to have to go and tell another family that their patriarch is never coming home, because I remember being on the receiving end of that conversation, and once I was old enough to really understand it, I remember it ripping apart every single little piece of my heart and soul – I can't do that to another person."

Harry was deflecting – I could hear it in his voice. He wanted to pretend that his problem was some desire not to hurt other people, and I'm sure on some level it probably was. But on a deeper, much more relevant level, he just missed his dad and had never really dealt with those emotions.

As Harry finished speaking, I reached out and held his hand, helping him brace for the questions and "support".

"You thought you were ok until that day?" Andrea questioned.

"I did," said Harry. "I mean, I knew I missed my dad, but I never saw it as something that would hold me back, especially not as a doctor. But I couldn't distance it from my mind. I did everything they told us not to do: I took it personally, got too attached and let that impact the quality of patient care. I haven't been back to class since that day. I missed the entire last week of lectures and labs. I know I have to when the new semester starts, but I don't know how to face that kind of failure again."

"In the emergency services training, they teach us the same thing," Dwayne said softly. Everyone turned to look at him. "They say don't get too attached, but, truth be told, if you

Limitations

don't, you become complacent and heartless. You aren't human if you don't feel the weight of trauma, especially when you lose the ones that are closest to you. The key is finding a balance between being invested and not too attached – feel the pain but don't let it bury you. That's what you learn on the job anyway," he finished with a small nod in Harry's direction. "And find someone who you can come home to at the end of the night, someone who makes the pain worth it, knowing you get to see their face again," Dwayne added, raising his eyebrows at my hand in Harry's.

Harry's hands squeezed mine tighter, and his rigid body softened beside me, but I was not in any way calm. The same fear I had held in my stomach all morning was taking over my entire body. My face warmed and my heart started to race, and quickly I excused myself to the bathroom.

Inside the bathroom stall, I stood with my back leaning against the door, eyes fixed on the graffitied words,

"Amelia Waz 'Ere", which must've been written at a time when speaking like that was considered cool.

I am no stranger to panic attacks and they do have a habit of sneaking up in my more vulnerable moments – when I'm hungover or haven't slept properly, for example. So, I know exactly how to bring myself down off the ledge when they get bad:

1. Find a quiet space with limited stimuli.

2. Lean up against a sturdy surface that supports my weight.

3. Find a spot on the opposite wall to focus on.

4. Take deep breathes, in through my nose for three seconds and out for five seconds.

5. Repeat step four for at least five minutes.

6. If symptoms persist, run.

Ok, admittedly, the final step is my own addition, but when all else fails – sometimes all I can do is run far

Limitations

away from all my triggers. I was five years old when I first experienced a panic attack, and like most people, I thought I was dying. Sometimes when I can't get them under control, I run in the literal sense. I throw on the closest shoes and just run through the city until I can't possibly run any longer. Sometimes I run to something that feels conversant, an old book or television series that provides comfort and familiarity. And sometimes I run away, which I'm not so proud of. This tendency got me in a lot of trouble in my early years of adulthood. One time I stole my mum's car and drove all the way to the Canadian border before I realised I had forgotten my passport and had to drive all the way back. I can't explain why I do these things. I guess it's one of those "the grass is always greener on the other side" type of situations, but when I do, for a few brief moments, the world doesn't feel like its crumbling around me.

Thankfully, today I was able to bring myself back to the ground. After about five minutes, I stepped out of the stall, washed my hands and wandered back to the room.

"You ok?" Harry asked softly as I took the seat beside him once again.

"Yeah, I'm fine," I lied, putting on my best fake smile. I settled in for the remainder of the day, but the ache in the pit of my stomach never fully settled.

Chapter 15

Harry and I walked out of the library with our hands intertwined as the harsh summer sun shone through the soft clouds. Beside me, Harry's steps were heavy. I could feel him leaning on me more than he had before. I could feel the weight of the last few hours pulling him down.

I felt the fear sitting in the pit of my stomach, threatening to take control once more. I wanted to hold on to him, to tell him that everything was going to be ok, but I didn't know how to do that when I didn't really believe it myself. So instead of telling him what I wasn't sure was true, I did the only thing I knew how to do – run – but with him by my side. I fought the urge to take us both to some remote destination and instead opted for an escape a little closer to home.

"You up for some unpublished treasures," I asked, letting go of his hand and turning to face him.

Harry's expression softened – the pain of the day lifting ever so slightly as he whispered, "There is nothing I want to do more."

Hand in hand, we headed to the train station and took off toward home. When we arrived at my stop, I took Harry into Ella Tienda. We stocked up on tubs of Ben and Jerry's and paid at the counter.

Inside the small dusty room in the basement, we sat on the floor, piles of manuscripts in our laps and a tub of ice cream in our hands.

"Listen to this," I said excitedly. "'Where the sky meets the sea, you will find me. For here, we will never need to say goodbye.' God, I would love to just run away to a beach or something! Somewhere where no one knows me and I don't have to answer to anything or anyone, somewhere I can just breathe."

I closed my eyes for a moment, picturing the beach from my dreams the night before. The feeling in the pit of my stomach fading slightly at the thought.

Harry's eyes darkened and his face turned so dark, so twisted that he seemed like a different person.

"People always think that the world is better the further they get from home," he said. "They think they can run away and it will solve all their problems, but all it does is cause more." He spoke with a sharpness that I had never heard out of him.

"I didn't mean it like that," I replied with a nervous laugh.

Harry stood, leaving the ice cream and the manuscripts on the floor beside me. With anger becoming more and more evident on his face, he stood over me, looking down.

"You did, though, because that's what you do, isn't it, Lilly? You run away when things get difficult so you don't have to face other people, so they don't have to see you struggling to stay afloat. As long as your problems don't drag you down, who cares what your absence might do to everybody else," he snapped, his voice rising with each word.

Shocked, and frankly a little annoyed, I got to my feet. "Woah, calm down, dude. There's no need to get all antagonistic." I said, raising my hands in surrender.

"You drive me nuts, you know that?" he yelled. "One minute you are here beside me reading books, the next you are a million miles away. I don't know how to win with you."

And in an instant, I was triggered, the rage inside of me spilled over the edge.

Limitations

"I'm not a prize," I yelled. "This isn't a competition that you can win, and no one is asking you to stick around! Just leave if you have such a problem with how I handle things." I pointed toward the closed door.

"That's what you'd prefer, isn't it?" he said firmly. "It's easier for you when there's no one around for you to lose."

"You got it in one. Now get the hell away from me!" I screamed, opening the door and pointing in the direction of the exit.

To my surprise, and disappointment, Harry listened immediately. He brushed past me, stormed out and slammed the door so hard behind him that it shook the shelves and sent dust flying into the air. I heard him stomping off down the hall and up the stairs to the main exit. He didn't stop once, he didn't even take a second to rethink his actions. He just continued on, his steps becoming quieter.

I sat back down on the floor. Tears streamed down my face, leaving small stains on the pages of the book I had been reading. The emotions that had built up inside of me had nowhere else to go, and the only thing I could do was cry. Because deep down he was right. I was so scared to lose anyone that I pushed them away before it got hard. What he didn't know was that when I said I wanted to run away, I didn't mean that I wanted to do it alone. When I pictured myself on a beach far away from everything, I pictured him lying in the sun beside me, his untidy hair blowing in the breeze. Was it healthy to run away? Probably not, but it was what I wanted, what I needed, and I sure as hell wasn't going to apologise for that.

I looked back down, and through teary eyes, I read the next line in the book: "But in the morning when I wake, it was all a dream. There's no such thing as fate."

Limitations

Dear Lilly,

Who would have guessed that it would end this way? Oh, that's right, you did. He was in a sensitive place. You knew that, yet you chose to say something like that anyway. This is your fault, and it's not because you're not good enough. It's because you don't know how to keep your goddamn mouth shut.

This is why it's easier not to feel anything – when you don't feel, you can't be hurt and you can't hurt other people. Just run away. It's what you want – it's what he wants. It would be better for everyone.

People fight. This could all be fine – you know that – so why does it feel like the end?

From Lilly

Chapter 16

I spent the earliest years of my life in a town called Wattle

Grove. It was a peaceful suburb in the heart of Western

Sydney. It's not a place many people know of, nor is it a

place many people choose to visit, but for a few short years

it was my entire world. The area is named after the acacia, or

wattle, trees, that line every strip of road in the area, filling

the streets with bright yellow flowers every autumn. I did

my first year of schooling in this tiny part of the world, at

the local public school. I was in the first kindergarten class

to start at the brand-new school, and my name is still written on a small, solid, green leaf on the fabricated wattle tree in the school's hall.

When Mum and I left Wattle Grove, I was too young to fully understand the magnitude of our move, but a little piece of me stays behind in that school, a reminder that I was once there, where my world fell apart over and over again. When you break, it's hard to fit the pieces back together again, and even when you do, there are always tiny fragments that never quite fit back into place. I miss that place sometimes – the woody smell of the wattle trees and the way the cars would race past our windows each night – but mostly I miss the me that I was before my world imploded.

When I woke up the next morning, I half-expected a message from Harry, something to prove that yesterday didn't happen or something that might take it all away. Instead, I was greeted by fourteen news alerts from around the world and two notifications from Instagram letting me know that a celebrity had gone live. I'm not going to pretend

I wasn't mad, that I wasn't hurt by it all, because the reality

is, it felt like someone had dropped a ten-pound weight on

my chest. It was all I could do to keep breathing in spite of

every force telling me to stop. I pulled my moleskin

notebook off my bedside table and tried to write something,

anything, that might relieve some of the weight, but nothing

came. Eventually, I wrote the words that were playing in my

mind like a song on repeat – the words that Harry had read

out to me that first day in the cupboard: *In your wake, you

left nothing but fragmented flowers, squashed into the

ground, forgotten and unrecognisable.*

It took a lot more strength than I knew I had to get

out of bed that day, but I did it, and I was strangely proud of

myself. Even as I dressed and walked to the train station, it

felt like some invisible force was holding me back, telling

me not to go, but I kept pushing through.

When I arrived, the room was almost empty. I sat in my original seat with my face buried in my phone as the others walked into the room. Harry was the last to arrive. I looked up at him for a second, but he turned his eyes away, and I returned my attention to the Buzzfeed quiz I had been engrossed in. He used to look at me like I hung the moon and stars just for him. And now I would give anything for him to look at me like that.

I didn't hear it properly at first, Andrea's soft voice was drowned out by the loudness in my head. When she spoke again, it shook me violently out of my own mind.

"Lilly," Andrea said in a gentle tone. "Would you like to share with us?" she asked.

My heart sunk as I heard the words. All the preparation, all the hours spent pouring through my past led to this moment. Now it was here, it was all I could do not to sink to the ground and cry. Did I have the option to say no? I mean, she did ask if I would like to share with the group –

Limitations

right? What would happen if I just said no? I didn't want to share every single part of me with a room full of strangers and the absolute best and most important person I had ever met.

I looked around the room, begging for someone to help me out of this, but every single one of them stared at me with the same blankness I had given them in the days before. All except for Harry, whose face looked shell-shocked. He didn't want to hear what I had to say and that was all on me. If I hadn't pushed him away, like I always did, he would be by my side, holding my hand and pulling me through all the bad stuff, like he always did.

With a deep breath, I reached down to my handbag that sat below my feet and pulled out my notebook.

I looked down at my "big list of nothing even remotely helpful", took another deep breath.

"I didn't lose anyone in the attack on the World Trade Center. I wasn't on a plane or throwing myself into burning buildings. I wasn't even in the country. I don't really have a place in this group. I don't deserve to be present in a room with all of you. I feel kind of useless when I think about all that each of you went through. I feel like there is something wrong with me. I feel like a sadist, living in the same pain and fear I had as a scared little girl. I don't know what to say here. I really don't. I don't know how to justify all my fears and worries. I don't know how to explain that I have this innate need to run from everything good and bad because I'm too afraid to feel. All I know for certain is that I need help."

I took another shaky breath and looked up from my notes.

"When ... when I was young, I lived in ... uh ... Syd ... Sydney," I stuttered, each word struggling more and more to leave my mouth.

The eyes of every person in that room broke their way through, shattering everything that had been holding me together for so long. My breathing became heavier and my heart rate sped up to an all-time high.

"I'm sorry ... I ... I can't do this," I cried, my voice cracking on the last word.

"It's ok to take your time, Lilly," Andrea reassured with a look of genuine concern.

As usual, Andrea had no idea what was going on. Though, if I'm honest, I'm not sure anyone in that room knew what was going on, not even me. I tried to fill my mind with happy thoughts, images of golden sand and deep blue seas, but they were quickly pushed out by all the darkness that was overcoming me. My heart beat so loudly I heard it in my ears. I tried to take deep breaths in through my nose, out through my mouth, but still I struggled to catch my breath. I looked around the room and saw nothing but the exit, and I knew what I had to do.

"I'm sorry," I cried out once more before picking up my bag and running out of the room.

As I ran down the hallway to the main staircase, I heard the faintest yell of my name. Even Harry wasn't going to be enough to bring me back though – nothing could do that. I needed to run far away until everything and everyone in that room was far behind me.

Limitations

Dear Lilly,

Ok, so you are doing this again. I mean, there are worse places to run to, but the ones that don't involve planes would be better. Yet here you are, thirty-six thousand feet above New York City, one hand gripped tightly around the armrest and the other holding this pen way too tightly.

I hope you know you proved Harry right by doing this. He told you all you do is run, and you ran ... good job. You are an intelligent person, but, goddamn it, you make terrible decisions sometimes.

If you actually make it to the Caribbean,

write again soon.

From Lilly

Chapter 17

When I was younger, we used to camp at this place somewhere down the coast from Sydney. I don't remember too much about it, except that it was close to the beach. There was an old rickety path, paved out of old logs, on the uneven sand. We would walk along this path, lined with overgrown shrubbery, until we came to a clearing that opened to a huge beach. We had picnics down at the waterside while the waves crashed violently against the shore. I could sit there for hours, mesmerised by the sound, building sandcastles in what the waves left behind. In the water, I would walk as far as my tiny body would allow, and then, when my feet could no longer touch the ocean floor, I would float, feeling the force of the waves shoot through my entire body. Then, as night grew darker, we'd pack up our picnic gear, head back along the path and settle into our tents for the night. I vividly remember the way I used to wrap the sleeping bag over my head because from afar there was something about the sound of the waves that scared the life out of me. They were the same waves I had stared at in bewilderment mere moments before, but now that they were out of sight, they were the cause of so much fear. Fear can be like that though. Seeing is understanding. When you can see the crashing waves, you know exactly what they are and how they work. When you can only hear them, there is nothing to stop you from thinking the worst. Nothing to stop you picturing them crashing down on top of you. Memories work in the same way. Sometimes, the memory of the darkest moments in your life scares you more than the actual event did.

Limitations

I could imagine the look on Harry's face – the look he would give me that screamed I told you so. I could see the way my mother would silently roll her eyes for days before she decided she would speak to me again. Ella would pretend, at least, that she was on my side, but deep down she would be disappointed that I had let my emotions take control. I just couldn't handle it anymore. I couldn't stand in front of them all and have every part of me pulled apart and examined under a microscope.

When I made that choice to run, I felt the pressure ease. It eased as I ran out of the building, as I jumped on the train toward home, as I packed my suitcase and as I stood in line at the airport waiting for my turn. By the time I boarded the plane, that room and all its pressures were way behind me. I was breathing normally again and focussing only on the path ahead.

I strolled along the long Jamaican shoreline, my feet gently pushing through the small waves that broke as they reached the shore. The soft, floral breeze blew gently on my face, and the summer sun shone on my back. A strange sense of peace, which I had not felt in years, filled every inch of my body. The truth of the matter was, that I wasn't at peace, not really. The nightmares would still haunt me – I would just wake up to a tropical breeze when they ended. I was still running, but now it was with the soft Caribbean sand beneath my feet instead of the hard New York sidewalk. This was a Band-Aid – it wouldn't help long term, but for a now, it felt like some of the pressure was off, some of the expectations taken away.

That was, of course, until I saw him at the other end of the beach. His blonde hair moved ever so slightly in the breeze. I stopped, dead in my tracks. Then I noticed him moving toward me. My eyes must have been playing tricks on me! They say when you miss someone, you see them everywhere, right? But this was different – he was actually there.

Limitations

"What the actual fuck are you doing here?" I yelled as he reached my side.

Harry, who had run in my direction after spotting me, was visibly out of breath. He held his hand up for a second, asking me to give him a moment to catch his breath. I stood still, frustrated, with one hand on my hip as the summer breeze blew my hair backwards.

"I might ... ask you ... the same ... question," Harry gasped, trying desperately to catch his breath as he spoke.

"You followed me to Jamaica?" I yelled. "Are you mental?"

"No, I absolutely did not!" he yelled straight back.

"Right, ok, so you just happened to show up on the same beach as me, one thousand miles from home?"

"I didn't follow you to Jamaica. I followed you home and waited at your front door. Eventually, your mum turned up and told me you had texted her from the airport. She was worried sick about you, so I told her I would go find you and bring you home," said Harry, his tone the same as when we fought the day before.

"You met my mother?" I yelled back at him.

Harry looked at me, an exhausted look on his face. He laughed, and I could tell he thought I was a complete fool. And all it did was make me furious.

"You are really taking the wrong things out of this story, Lil," he said, with an exasperated laugh.

"Don't you dare laugh at me. I left that group. I left you for a reason. What gives you the right to come here and act like the hero?" I yelled again.

Harry looked straight at me for a few moments, his body rigid, a maddened look on his face.

"Don't act like you're the only one who has ever been hurt," he said. "I see you, remember? I see your pain. I know you think you can do this on your own – and you know what, you probably can – but I'm not going to leave you in fucking Jamaica and go home without you. If you want to do this, if this is the way you get your closure, fine, but I'm not gonna let you do it alone. I left you in that closet and that was completely on me. I was too scared you were going to run away when I needed you. I was selfish and upset and I made a mistake, ok?" He yelled in a way that seemed to contradict every word he was saying.

"You nailed it the other day," I said, tears forming in the corner of my eyes. "I'm scared that things will fall apart, so I run away before they do! The only good things in my life, that haven't abandoned me, are the ones I abandoned before they got the chance to. I'm alone and I'm scared as all hell, and the last thing I want to do is fuck this up. But I know me, so just leave while you have a chance."

"Hey," Harry yelled, his voice reaching a volume I wasn't aware he was capable of. "You don't own Jamaica. You can't banish me. If I want to have a relaxing holiday here, I freaking can." But then his expression changed. His body relaxed and he whispered, "I'm not leaving you here or anywhere." He was so certain in the way he spoke, as if it was a fact that I should have already known.

My breath hitched in my throat, and I watched his eyes, those eyes I had come to love so much over the last two weeks.

"Look at where we are," he said, lifting his arms up as if to put the gorgeous beach on display. "I flew three and a half hours to come here and tell you that you don't have to do this alone. Do you think you yelling at me is going to make me go home? Yell at me all you want, but I'm still gonna be here for you," he shouted.

I didn't know what to do or say or think.

"You keep trying to push me away because it's easier for you that way. I know it's only been two weeks since we met, but I see you, and you don't strike me as the kind of person to give up, so don't start now. You don't need to do this on your own. You don't need to shut me out just to feel better," he reassured sternly.

Limitations

With a shaky breath, I yelled back the only thought I was capable of thinking, "I don't need you to save me."

Harry exhaled, dropping his arms to his side and tilting his head like a confused dog. "I don't want to save you," he said calmly. "That's your job, and I would never dare get in your way. I just want to hold your hand while you save yourself."

My mind reeled at the words as they left his mouth. It was unimaginable to believe that anyone would bother to fly all this way to help me – even my own mother outsourced it. But here he stood, ready to take on whatever crazy adventure I had planned if it meant it would make me feel better. I took a deep breath, lowered my hand from my hip and let my body soften in the summer sun.

"If you really mean that, it means you're signing up to completely ignore our problems for a few days and just live," I whispered softly and uncertainly.

Harry stepped forward and wrapped his arms around me in a tight embrace. I resisted at first but then softened and wrapped my arms tightly around his back, a solitary tear leave my eye.

"What problems?" he whispered in my ear.

I let a soft laugh escape and quickly pulled myself out of the hug. Another small tear ran down my face as we began to walk up the beach, the waves continuing to break ever so gently around my feet.

Chapter 18

I had always been a city girl. I liked the proximity, the ability to be quickly in the heart of it all, and I had become used to drowning out the sounds of the traffic every morning. But there was nothing in this world I despised more than the rush, the feeling that everyone around me had somewhere to be and that I was just a roadblock in the way. Getting away resettled me, reminding me of what was really important. Nature had this incredible way of calming me down – there's something comforting in knowing that there is this massive force that operates completely on its own without any intervention needed. When all in the world feels lost, the sun will still rise tomorrow and the waves will still crash against the shore.

As the afternoon approached, we sat together on the crowded beach, the harsh sun piercing our skin. I took deep breaths, watching the waves as they moved in and out on the shore.

I felt Harry beside me; his breath was calm and his mind was working. He wanted to say something – I could feel it – but I was in no rush to push him. I listened as he inhaled sharply, his breath hitching in his throat.

"So, uh, I may or may not have read your letters," Harry murmured shakily.

My mind raced. "I'm sorry, you did what?" I snapped at him.

Harry raised his hands in surrender and laughed. "Please don't start yelling at me again," he requested. "I didn't realise what they were at first, and by the time I did, I genuinely couldn't stop."

Limitations

I took a deep breath, trying to calm myself down. I picked up tiny handfuls of sand and let them slowly seep out of my hands. "What did you think?" I said.

"That we are a lot more alike than I thought," whispered Harry, making the exact same motion with the sand.

I smiled slightly and then placed my hands underneath my body. "How so?" I queried.

Harry stopped fiddling with the sand and turned his body to face me.

"We were both too young to deal with that kind of loss. We were both emotionally stunted at the age we lost our fathers, and we both blame someone who is just as much the victim as we are. But deep down, there is nothing wrong with us – we are just scared kids who feel alone in this massive world," he replied with a smile.

I didn't really know how to respond, so I took a deep breath and looked out to sea, resting my head on his shoulder. This beautiful human, this absolute force of a man, had interpreted my scribble list of emotions, better than any psychologist ever had, and summed me up in just a few lines.

"It's all inside of you, Lilly," said Harry. "It all comes out when you write. You don't have to run away anymore; this world is a scary place, but it's easier if we face it together."

My mouth was dry, my eyes heavy and my body weak. I felt like I had run a marathon without so much as a five-second break for a drink of water. I fought the urge to scream at him for reading something so personal, knowing deep down that he only had the best intentions.

"Never read anything I write again without my permission," I said. It may have been a little harsh, but I think he got the point.

Limitations

We didn't say anything for quite a while. We just sat in each other's presence, staring out to sea, fiddling with the sand and feeling the soft summer breeze on our faces.

"I hired a car to get here from the airport, it's not the most reliable – like it may quite literally fall apart at any second. But ... I was thinking that we could drive to this beach I saw on the way here? Apparently, there is a beachside restaurant there where you can get fresh seafood and eat it on tables in the water," Harry gushed excitedly. "Please tell me you like seafood?"

I smiled at his enthusiasm and the thought of fresh seafood warming me up from the inside out.

"I call dibs on driving music." I jumped to my feet and reached out my hand, helping him to his feet. Harry's face was so bright that it illuminated every dark part of the day. It is a scientific fact that human bodies give off the tiniest amount of light that is too weak for the eye to see. But when I looked at him, in that moment, I swear to god I saw it.

Harry wasn't wrong in his warnings about the car. It was a 1995 Toyota Tacoma truck that looked like it hadn't been serviced or cleaned in the twenty-six years since it was made. The entire thing was covered in cobwebs and old leaves. When I opened the passenger-side door, hundreds of baby spiders crawled out onto my hands and all over the truck. I screamed at the top of my lungs, jumping around and shaking my hands in a desperate attempt to get them off me. Harry offered no help. He laughed louder than ever.

"Laugh all you want, but if I find the mother anywhere in this car, it will find itself on your head." I glared at him.

He looked across the top of the truck with an apologetic smile and a cheeky wink.

I plugged my phone into the USB cable hanging from the brand new radio, probably the only upgrade this car had had, and hit shuffle. As we drove, we sang and danced in our seats to the songs that came through the dodgy sound system, and we laughed at tourists on the side of the road. One woman we drove past was running from one side of a field to another as a goat ran around behind her, its head bowed, ready to "attack". We laughed so hard that Harry had to pull over to compose himself before he could continue driving.

"Do you ever feel like a song just perfectly sums up exactly how you feel?" I asked as "Hurricane" from the musical *Hamilton* played loudly through the car speakers.

"I do, yeah," said Harry. "I just hope the title isn't foreshadowing anything – we are in the Caribbean after all." He laughed as he pointed at the title on the radio's small screen.

"Oh god, it'd be just our luck, wouldn't it?" I laughed.

I smiled at the bright green trees and deep blue oceans that filled the distance. Harry had come this far just for me, and despite everything, he was still by my side. I listened intently to the lyrics and allowed them to fill me up.

By the time we arrived at the other beach, the sun was starting to set. Harry opened the door for me, saving me from any spiders that had survived the trip. He took my hand and led me down the beach to a small rustic hut where we ordered a small seafood platter and took our seats on tables just a few inches under water.

All around us, the sun began to set, birds circled overhead and the waves rushed softly up our legs. I looked around at this picture-perfect place and felt nothing but pure calm. I knew it wouldn't last forever, but I didn't care. I exhaled and picked up a prawn from the platter.

Harry struggled to remove the shell from his own prawn, so I leaned across the table, showing him a trick that my grandfather had taught me years before.

Limitations

"I am really happy you're here," I whispered.

He leaned forward, placing a soft kiss on my cheek.

It was late by the time we returned to the hotel. I lay awake for a while, writing and watching Harry sleeping beside me. By the time I decided to sleep, I was so tired that I crashed out the second my head hit the pillow, my nightmares replaced by peaceful dreams of sunsets and the best seafood I had ever had.

Dear Lilly,

You're for real, aren't you- Harry Crawford?

This crazy force of a human has absolutely blown me away today. In this moment, I truly believe that there is nothing so bad in this world that can't be fixed with a walk on the beach and a seafood dinner. And Harry is responsible for every single shred of that belief. When he sleeps, his eyelids flutter ever so slightly. For now, I am ok to sit there, watching him breathe. Sometimes it's ok to just be.

Love Lilly

Chapter 19

They say that when you meet the person you're going to spend the rest of your life with, you will just know. What they don't mention is, how completely insane you will think you are when you feel this way. Suddenly you become infatuated by their every movement. You picture a life with them and desperately want nothing more than to spend more time with them. Yep ... you feel completely mental, and god forbid you mention it to your friends. They don't know that feeling, they don't understand what it's like – hell, I can't even really put it into words! They don't know what it feels like to see your entire world reflected in the eyes of a person who you hardly even know, and they don't know what it's like to stand in the mirror, trying to talk yourself down. They don't know what it's like to lie awake at night, hoping and praying that that person saw the same thing when they looked at you. I can't explain it, but when I heard Harry's passion, his enthusiasm, when I saw the pain hiding behind his hypnotic eyes – I just knew – I wouldn't love another person for my entire life. Like a drug, I was hooked.

*

The sun poured through our open blinds when we woke the next morning. It was so late that we'd missed our designated timeslot for breakfast and had to sweet-talk our way into a later session. Thankfully, we were successful, and we ate more mini banana pancakes than is considered socially acceptable – so many that we spent what was left of the morning lying on beach chairs, giving in to our food-induced coma.

It was a good hour of lying in the sun before I remembered something I had read on the activities board earlier that morning: "See the wild side of the island – 12:00pm today". I sat upright and checked the time on my smart watch – 11:50am. I jumped to my feet.

"So, um ..." I said coyly.

Harry looked shaken. "Oh god, that's not the start of anything sane, when it comes to you." Apprehensively, he stood.

"Oh, come on, sanity is so overrated." I laughed. "There's something I wanted to do this afternoon – would you care to join me?" I said with a cheeky smile.

"In the future, I will have nightmares about that very face." Harry laughed, pointing at me.

"Come on, it's an adventure – embrace it!" I laughed.

Harry rolled his eyes, relaxed his body and held out his hand for me to take. This was the best part about Harry – I could suggest the wildest things, and he would still go along with it without much of a second thought.

I grabbed his hand, and together we walked toward a hut about 100 metres away from the beach.

"You're not even going to tell me where we are going?" Harry asked nervously as I dragged him along.

"I could ... but what would be the fun in that?"

I managed to hide the nature of our big adventure, even as we waited in line at the activities hut and signed out our equipment. Though Harry did seem more and more hesitant with each step.

As we stood on the side of the wild river, a tour guide stood in front of us, giving his safety demonstration.

"White-water rafting!" he yelled in my ear.

"Relax, man, we'll be fine," I whispered back to him.

Limitations

Harry looked me up and down for a second, as if he was trying to decipher something, and then, with the most sincere look of concern, he asked, "You have a death wish, don't you?"

"Nope, I just feel it's about time we start living our lives," I whispered back, matter-of-factly. As I spoke, the tour guide finished his safety demonstration and instructed us all to select a raft and get started. I faced Harry, who remained frozen in his place on the riverbank. "Correct me if I'm wrong, but I believe it was you who told me that," I continued, louder this time.

He rolled his eyes.

"Do you not agree?" I asked with another cheeky smile.

Harry moved forward, and jokingly pushed me toward the rapid river. "Stop with that damn face." He laughed.

Together, we selected the closest red raft. We climbed on board, which was not a simple task, given the way the water was thrashing around. Once we were secure in the raft, the tour guide released the rope that was holding us in place, and we rapidly soared away from the shore. Harry jumped. He shoved his oar straight down into the water, stabbing the river floor and making the entire boat jerk.

"Are we actually doing this?" he yelled at me over the sound of the thrashing water.

"Take a leap, man. Let's start living!" I laughed. Harry still seemed uncertain. "I know it's scary, but isn't that what makes it so incredible?" The waves buffeted us around, splashing water all over our heads. "Come on, for the rest of our lives we will be able to say that we had this amazing experience, and I don't know about you, but I would rather that than to be that person who says I almost did this." I watched Harry's face change as he considered what I had said. "You also need to get the oar off the ground now or we'll tip over!"

With a nervous smile and a shaky breath – which was somehow audible above the sound of the water – Harry pulled his oar out of the ground and back into the boat. We shot down the rapid river, the boat giving in to the current of the water.

In the distance, the tour guide yelled, "You won't be able to do that trick later!"

I wasn't entirely sure what that meant, but it did cause Harry to whip his head around to look at me.

"That's not ominous at all," he yelled, his eyes wide.

Chapter 20

Harry was this bizarre exception to every rule I'd ever made. We never had that awkward "will they, won't they" stage. It felt predestined, like it didn't really matter what we did, we were always going to end up together. We also never had a conversation about it. We never felt this weird need, that people our age typically feel, to define ourselves. We didn't make anything Facebook official. We didn't call each other boyfriend/girlfriend. We were the way we were, and we never questioned it.

This was good in so many ways, but it also meant that in those early days I never got a chance to tell him so many things that I should have said. I never mentioned that when I looked into his eyes, I saw my entire world reflected back at me. I didn't tell him that from the minute we met I simply couldn't imagine a future without him in it. It's probably for the best because I really don't know how to put into words the way he makes me feel. What else could I say? He's not perfect, but, oh my god, he is so incredibly perfect.

Our tiny raft slammed into rocks, shaking our bodies around at unnaturally high speeds, and it was well into the evening by the time we emerged from the rapids. The water had calmed significantly and the setting sun was reflected in the water ahead. Taking Harry's lead, I pulled my oar out of the water, allowing us to float along at a relaxing pace. He turned around carefully on the raft to face me.

"I don't know what you were so scared of – that was fun!" he said, laughing.

"Oh yeah," I sniggered. "I was scared, Mr Death Wish."

"In my defence," he said, "that was quite literally the most adventurous thing I have ever done."

I laughed. "Is that really a defence?" I reached my hand over the side of the raft and splashed him with the warm water.

"You'll pay for that!" Harry chuckled.

In an instant, I was tipped out of the raft and into the water, clothes and all. The water was a shock to my system, but it was warm, surrounding my body like a hug from an old friend.

I treaded water as I yelled up to him, "You suck so much! You better get your ass in here!"

Harry stood, struggling to keep his balance on board the raft, and laughed at me.

"Never," he yelled back. But in the same instant, he lost his balance and came toppling headfirst into the water beside me.

"Justice!" I yelled out when he finally surfaced.

Limitations

"Oh yeah." He laughed, grabbing on to me and pushing me down until my head was beneath the surface.

Kicking and laughing, I fought against him, attempting to push him beneath the surface, until he stopped ... his eyes wide with shock.

My heart stopped. "What?"

Assuming there must have been some awful river shark or some Jamaican variation of the Loch Ness Monster behind me, I whipped my body around in the water to see ... nothing. Instead, I felt his arms on either side of me, turning me back around to face him.

Then he kissed me hard on the lips. It caught me off guard, but I gave in, kissing him back with everything I had in me. I wrapped my legs around his back to keep us from drifting apart, and we floated there for what felt like a lifetime.

It must have been a good minute before I opened my eyes and realised that there was no one else around. The rest of our tour group had drifted much further along the river, around a bend, and were now out of sight. This would have been fine, of course, if our raft hadn't drifted away with them.

"So?" Harry questioned, looking blankly at the water around us.

"I hope you can swim," I said before dipping my head under the water and swimming off in the direction of our raft and the rest of our tour group.

"Too bad if I can't," I heard Harry yell out, muffled through the sound of the water rushing past my ears.

We swam for a few hundred metres and finally caught up with our raft, which was trapped by a rock sticking up through the water's surface. Then we paddled for the rest of the tour. By the time we arrived at the end, my arms felt like jelly and all I wanted to do was sleep.

*

Limitations

That night, we sat around a small beach fire, mesmerised by the crackling logs. While the waves continued to crash against the shore, we drank cocktails from cups shaped like coconuts, and Harry sat as close to me as was humanly possible.

I rested my head on his shoulder. "Have you ever sat and watched the sea crash over rocks? It's kind of like us, isn't it?" I asked, listening to the sea crash in the distance.

Harry looked at me, bewilderment spreading across his face. "I don't know how to take that."

"We were thrust by the same force into the hardest place," I said. "We were thrown around, shaken up, and yet we still managed to find each other when the water washed back out to sea."

Harry smiled at my complete nonsense as if he knew exactly what I meant, even when I wasn't entirely sure I did.

"You know we have to go back right," he whispered.

"Why?" I joked. "We could stay here forever. Who would know?" Then I thought better of it, and with a deep breath I said, "I know. I've already booked a flight for both of us tomorrow morning." I wanted it to be a lie more than anything, but it wasn't. "We have to face the things that are holding us back, don't we?"

"We do, Lilly. This running, it's only—"

"A Band-Aid." I shrugged.

"We're stronger if we do it together." Harry smiled before standing and pulling me up beside him. "But tonight, it's just you and me, and the rest of the world doesn't matter."

As we walked along the beach toward the resort cabin, I made fun of Harry's cheesy expressions. When we arrived back, I got dressed into pyjamas and smiled at him standing shirtless on our balcony reading something on his phone.

As I strolled gently toward him, a soft music hit my ears – it was a song I had never heard before, but it was beautiful. Harry reached for my hand, and when I grabbed his, he pulled me into his body. In the warm night air, we danced in one another's arms as the song ran on a loop, "There goes my mind, racing, and you are the reason that I'm still breathing." The lyrics took a place inside my heart, where they would stay forever.

When the song ended, I stayed with my arms wrapped tightly around Harry's neck and my head buried in his chest until he pulled away and placed a soft kiss on my forehead.

"We'll be ok, Lilly," he whispered. "I can promise you that much. Nothing is so bad that we can't get through it together."

I smiled up at him. The waves crashed violently in the distance, but I wasn't afraid, I felt more peaceful than I have ever thought possible.

Limitations

Dear Lilly,

You are strong. You have done something today that you never thought possible. You are in love, even if you aren't ready to admit it yet. Tomorrow you have to face a new day back in the real world, a break from your fantasies, and you will be ok. It's not going to be easy. It could be one of the hardest things you ever do, but it will be alright.

"I don't wanna cry no more ... you are the reason."

Love Lilly

Chapter 21

When Harry and I returned from Jamaica on Sunday morning, my mother was waiting at the airport. She was happy to see us at first, and faked a smile for the whole car ride until we dropped Harry off home to his anxious mother. It wasn't until we arrived home that Mum cracked. For a good five hours straight, she yelled about how inconsiderate and selfish I had been to leave with nothing but a text. I screamed back. We slammed doors and threw cushions until we both gave up and went to bed without another word. I spent the next day in my bedroom, only emerging to use the bathroom or to grab something from the kitchen – each time ignoring her tuts and muttered complaints.

It was Tuesday before I next spoke to Mum.

"We need milk," I muttered, slamming the empty container onto the sink.

"You could get some," she replied with a shake of her head and a not-so-subtle eye roll.

I didn't have the energy for another huge argument, so instead I poured my tea into a keep cup, tied my messy hair into a ponytail, grabbed my handbag off the countertop and walked swiftly out of the apartment. For once, I was looking forward to heading into support group.

*

"How was the rest of your weekend?" Harry asked as I entered the room and took the seat next to him.

"Don't be an ass." I laughed, knowing full well that he knew just how bad my Sunday was from our late-night call and text chains.

Harry had also received a fair amount of yelling to round out the weekend. His mum wasn't exactly on board with him running off to another country for "some girl".

It was hurtful. I didn't want her to hate me as much as she clearly did before I even got the chance to meet her, but I certainly understood.

The tenth and final member of the group, Josh, took the stage to tell his story. Josh was a pilot. He had been over Louisiana when word came over the radio that America was under attack. He remained cool, calm and collected as he landed at the New Orleans International Airport. He comforted scared and confused passengers as they sat on the plane for over thirteen hours, waiting for their turn to pass the upgraded security measures. He remained strong despite his fear that one of his passengers could've been involved in the attack and could've endangered the lives of everyone on board. It wasn't until much later that he allowed himself to fall apart. For weeks, he didn't return to the air, and when he did, it wasn't the same place he had known and loved. It was tainted with fear. The whole thing came to a head when a flight attendant accidentally opened the cockpit door mid-flight. Josh had a massive panic attack that led to a mayday call and a sudden loss of altitude. After this, Josh resigned, and he hadn't returned to the sky.

"The thing is, being pilot was the only thing I ever really loved," said Josh. "The minute I realised I wanted to be a pilot, my life had direction, and I lost it all in one day. I just want to go home," he said, his eyes transfixed on the wall opposite him.

Josh was scared. You could see it in every gesture. The plane had been his happy place, his home, and someone flew in and destroyed it. How do you move on when the only home you've ever known is not the same safe place you thought it was?

Later that day, Harry and I walked toward the subway station. Harry chattered about the day, but my head was elsewhere. I had given nothing more than a few word responses to everything he had said for the last five minutes.

Harry extended his arm out in front of me.

"Ok, what's up?" he asked.

I stopped walking.

"Noth—"

"Don't even try it," Harry snapped playfully.

Harry led me over to a nearby park bench and we sat together, the hot afternoon sun shining through the leaves on the trees above.

"Come on," he prodded.

"I don't know," I said. "I guess I just get scared sometimes."

Limitations

I felt Harry's eyes on me, but I kept my eyes fixed intently on my own hands.

"Of anything in particular?" he asked.

I thought about lying to him, giving him some half-baked excuse, but what would be the point? I had come so far. I wanted help. I needed help. I wouldn't get anywhere hiding from my fears. Besides, he could read me like a book.

"I get scared when I think about how close we could be to complete disaster and not even know it," I whispered.

Harry sighed. Then, ever so quietly, he laughed. I looked up at him, puzzled.

"Lilly," he said. "I'm going to tell you something now, and it might seem harsh, but it's important that you hear it."

I nodded, unsure what to expect.

"You are not special. We are all scared of the fragility of life. Some of us are just better at hiding it than others." Harry gently placed a hand on my cheek. "Life is fragile, yes," he said. "But isn't that what makes it so damn incredible?"

I tilted my head and leaned into his hand, giving him a look that said what the hell are you talking about?

"We could be dead tomorrow," Harry said gently. "That is what reminds me every single day to get up and keep living."

"I don't know how to do that," I said. "I'm trying, but it's not always that simple."

"I know," he whispered. "It takes some practice."

The truth is, this particular thought had been plaguing me ever since my dad left. The impossible reality that in a second everything could change and nothing would ever be the same. When you realise that at such a young age, it's impossible not to be afraid. I've spent my life questioning whether it's worth building a life when it can all be taken away in an instant.

Limitations

Harry tightly wrapped his arms around my shaking body and whispered in my ear, "The end isn't always the end, Lilly. Even when it feels like nothing will ever be the same, like you are so far broken that you can't be repaired, there is always a way through the darkness, back into the light. But you have to fight for it."

When I heard those words, something clicked inside of me, and I knew what I needed to do. If I ever wanted answers, I needed to stop waiting for them to fall in my lap. I needed to go looking for them. I needed to find my way back into the light.

"I'm going to go," I whispered to Harry, pulling out of his embrace.

"You ok?" he asked, quickly jumping into damage-control mode.

"I have some thoughts in my head, and I just need some time alone," I said softly.

"Ok," Harry responded hesitantly.

"I'm not running, I swear." I assured him.

"Sometimes when I say I need to be alone, it's because I really do – this is one of those times."

"Ok," he said again, but he was more certain this time.

I hugged Harry goodbye and headed toward to the subway station, my thoughts running more wild with every step.

Chapter 22

It was late into the afternoon by the time I got home. Without even setting my handbag down, I walked straight to Mum's room. In her wardrobe, she kept a storage container of old photo albums and documents. I had seen the photo albums millions of times, but there was always one she wouldn't let me touch. I knew what was inside, so I didn't ask any questions. She didn't want me to go through the pain of seeing the photos of a loving father before it all fell apart, and I had been in no rush to remember the way he used to look at me. But this day was different – I needed an explanation. I needed to see something that showed me he had always been that way, that it wasn't my fault.

I opened the photo album hesitantly. On the first page, there was a photo of me in a green basin. I'm three weeks old, and my dad's hands hold my tiny head out of the water. A few pages later, there was one of me on my first day of school, dressed in an oversized green and white checked uniform, smiling brightly in the late summer sun. Our ginger cat is sprawled out on the grass behind me. I'm not sure why Mum kept this one hidden, maybe it reminded her of something she'd rather forget or maybe it was the outline of my father's shadow on the ground in front of me. Either way, I liked it. It reminded me of a simpler time, of pretending that our cat was a crocodile and I was some weird female version of Steve Irwin who captured and saved him. Carefully, I peeled back the plastic cover and removed the photograph from its place in the book. I knew there was almost no chance that Mum looked through these albums, so

Limitations

I was certain she wouldn't miss it. I carefully placed the photo onto the floor beside me and turned back to the book. Where the photo had been, stuck to the page, was a tiny blue piece of paper, folded in two. It was brittle, but I was able to gently unfold it.

My heart rate shot up as I read what had been etched on the paper: *Michael – 2 Badgerys Road, Wattle Grove. 0449999679*

For twenty years, my mother had told me she had absolutely no clue where my father was and no way to contact him, but here she was, with an address and a mobile number hidden in a book full of baby photos.

My whole body shook, disbelief making way for anger and questions that I desperately needed answers to. I pulled my phone out of the back pocket of my jeans and dialled the number.

"Hello, Michael speaking," he said in a deep voice through the line.

In most situations, I try to remain level-headed, calculated and in control, but it wasn't until I heard his voice that I finally considered the ramifications of the call I was making. Mum would kill me. Any relationship we may have had left after my little 'vacation' would certainly be destroyed; I'd probably have to find somewhere else to live, move to another city where I could afford the rent and leave everything I know and love behind. I could have hung up the phone, hid the note, returned the photograph and left Mum's room as if none of it ever happened, but something in me told me to ignore all that, to push on, get the answers I have needed for so long.

"Hi," I responded abruptly.

"Can I ask who's calling?" he said hesitantly.

"Um, my name is Lilly," I said, hoping that he would catch on, but of course he didn't seem to. "Lilly Dempsey," I finished, certain this would ring the bell.

Limitations

He gasped. Then I heard what sounded like a door sliding, footsteps, then a door sliding and clicking into place.

"Oh my god, Lilly, how are you?" he whispered.

So that's how we were going to play this, I thought – let's act like old friends, pretend that it's totally normal for a father to have not once spoken to his daughter in twenty years. So I played along. I answered his questions, told him my exam scores and my biggest achievements and revealed we lived in New York. He seemed confused about how the girl with a perfect SAT score and a first place trophy in every spelling bee she'd ever competed in, at twenty-five, now worked in a convenience store with no degree to her name. I wanted to explain – tell him that it was all because of him – but what good would it do? I found out I had twin half-siblings, both of whom were at university studying science. I found out that he had established himself as a prominent Sydney business owner and that he was happily married to his wife of twenty-one years.

"Are you rounding up there?" I asked gently.

"No," he responded hesitantly. "We were married on June 21, 2001," he finished, like he was proud of it, like he thought I had forgotten the day he left.

"You left us ..." I said, my voice shaking so much that I couldn't finish my sentence.

He exhaled sharply.

"I know," he whispered, "and I'll regret it for the rest of my life."

And with that, I snapped. Every part of me that had fought the urge, for so many years, to find him and scream at him gave up, and I cracked.

"You left us on the 11th of September, 2001, three goddamn months after your wedding day to another woman?!" I screamed. "What happened, Dad, did you think I'd forget the date my entire world fell apart?"

"Now, Lilly," he began, his tone nothing but condescending.

Limitations

"No, no, no!" I screamed back. "Don't you dare use that tone with me! Don't you dare choose this moment to start acting like a father. Did you ever try to get in touch with me? Did you ever so much as try to make it work with Mum? Or did you just run away to your other family and screw everyone else who came before them? No, you know what, don't answer that. I don't want to know." My anger rose more and more with each second that passed.

"Lilly ... honestly, no, I didn't try, and that's on me," he said softly.

"Of course it's on you, idiot! Who else would it be on?"

My heart raced. I quickly covered the phone speaker and screamed at the top of my lungs, so loud that it scared a bird that had perched on our windowsill. All these years I had blamed Mum. I thought that if she hadn't have moved us so far away, then he might have been able to find us. But now I know she wasn't hiding me from him, she was protecting me. She was giving me a scapegoat. She was allowing herself to be the bad guy so I wouldn't feel like I deserved less. And then, for the first time, it occurred to me that he hadn't just left me, he had left her. I wondered how long he was planning on keeping the charade up; I wondered if I hadn't lost my mind so gloriously that day, if it hadn't been so hard, would he have kept it up? Would he ever have let her know, or would he have just continued playing his game?

"I'm going to hang up this phone now," I said sternly. "But before I do, I need to ask something of you."

"Ok?" he questioned.

"I have spent so much time blaming myself for you leaving, but I'm done with that now. Any father who can't deal with his daughter's distress in the wake of one of the worst tragedies in human history has absolutely no business being a father. I'm going to make something of myself. This isn't going to be the last time you hear my name, and I will make damn sure of that. So, I ask that you do three things: 1. Never speak to me again. 2. Never treat another human being the way you treated Mum and I, and 3. When I do make something of myself, when you hear my name again, you will claim absolutely no credit for it," I finished, the anger I had been feeling making space for clarity.

"I ..." he whispered.

"No, don't even bother saying anything else. I'm done." I removed my phone from my ear and hung up, slamming it down on the floor.

As I did so, I heard the front door close abruptly. I considered cleaning up the mess, but I thought better of it, and instead I pushed everything off my lap, jumped to my feet and ran out of Mum's room into the kitchen. There stood my mum, fed up, after a day at work, and evidently still angry with me. But she was still my mum, the woman who had moved her entire life for me, who had given me everything for twenty-five years, who had never once let on that she was going through the unimaginable. I ran straight to her, wrapped my arms tightly around her. Mum was thrown off guard as I cried apologies in her ear over and over and over again.

When we broke apart, she gently wiped a tear from my cheek.

"It's ok, Lilly, it's ok," she whispered. "All I wanted was a call, some sort of explanation, not just a text."

"No, Mum. I'm sorry about Dad," I whispered.

I told Mum about the photos and the phone call with Dad, and she explained to me that she had known for some time before Dad left that he was with someone else, but she didn't want to admit it. She apologised for not telling me the full story, and I apologised for everything I had ever done to make her feel like a bad parent – from crying at bedtime to not going to college. Mum told me that she never wanted me to go to college if it wasn't what I wanted; she didn't mind if I spent my entire life in a dead-end job so long as it was what I wanted – not just what I felt I deserved. I confessed that it was never what I wanted. I told her I always wanted to write and shared some short stories I'd thrown together in the past. I felt supported, and for the first time in a long time, I felt understood.

I wasn't ok. I wouldn't be for quite some time, but I could see a way out of all the darkness that had been filling my life for so long. I think deep down every member of the support group felt that they didn't deserve a place to grieve, but what no one ever told any of us was that there is no timeline or framework for things like this. We all have a right to feel like the world ended that day, because even for the healthiest of people, it seemed like it did.

I never imagined that speaking to my Dad would help. I pictured a *Notebook*-style reunion where Dad would reveal he'd written a letter every day since he'd left, and that I hadn't received them because he'd been unable to find me or because Mum had received them and kept them hidden.

What I got was nothing of the sort; what I got was more heart-breaking than I imagined, but inside all that pain I got a closure I had never thought possible.

Later on, I spoke to Harry on video chat. I unpacked the conversation and opened up to him about how relieved I was to no longer blame myself for something so damaging. He smiled at me. He smiled like I had finally gotten to his favourite part of the movie – he knew all along that I'd get there and had been waiting patiently for it to happen. His beautiful smile was so laced with pride that it filled me up in ways I never thought to be possible – the feeling would stay with me forever.

Chapter 23

No one tells you that working through trauma can be just as physically exhausting as it is mentally. By Friday morning of the third week of group, I felt like I had run a marathon. Despite desperately wanting to stay curled up in my bed, I fought through and pulled myself up. With the minimal energy I had left in me, I grabbed an old t-shirt and pair of shorts out of a drawer, pulled on a pair of aging light pink Keds, which had been sitting beside my bed for weeks, and threw my cardigan inside my handbag. Then I tied my hair up loosely and walked out of my room, not bothering to put any make-up on. Grabbing an apple from the bench, I left through the front door with a wave to Mum, who was busily

getting herself ready.

As I walked toward the station, I was overwhelmed

by a familiar smell. It was a flower or maybe a tree? I

couldn't put my finger on it, but it reminded me of those first

few years in Australia, of games played in the street and

running home before the sun set. It took me back to a time

before everything changed. So, I stopped for a moment and

breathed in deeply, cherishing the nostalgia that came along

with that scent. It's amazing how closely linked our

memories are to scent. In one tiny breath, we can be

transported far away to another time.

Outside the library, I noticed a rather large group of

people, most with headphones, standing around someone

wearing the most offensively bright yellow t-shirt. A tourist

group, I deduced, when one member of the group raised his

hand to, presumably, ask a question. This was not an

uncommon occurrence. The library was a must-see landmark

for travellers from all over the world. What was unusual, was the man on the far end of the group. He seemed uninspired and disconnected – he looked a lot like me on my first day of support group! He opted to not wear headphones, which could have meant he spoke English and didn't need them, but something about him made me think it had more to do with his utter disinterest. The man wore an oversized sweatshirt, which must have been excruciatingly hot in the New York Summer, and had a large backpack slung over one shoulder. If I'm being honest, he scared me a bit – there was something in his vacant expression and the cold way he stared through the library's open doors that sent a shiver up my spine.

"It's nothing," I whispered to myself.

But a tiny voice in the back of my head suggested the backpack was dodgy! I read something the other week about the size of those improvised explosive devices. A backpack would be just the right size.

This was a little game that my anxiety and I liked to play: it would try its damn hardest to convince me that seemingly harmless things were a potential threat, and I would work in overdrive trying to prove it wrong. My anxiety usually won, of course. You know in those kids shows, where someone's making a big decision and they put a tiny cartoon devil and angel on each of the person's shoulders to anthropomorphise the good and bad parts of their subconscious? That's basically my anxiety – except it's just the devil, and he's living inside my head, and he will not shut up under any circumstances.

As I made my way into the library, someone grabbed on to my shoulders abruptly.

I jumped.

Harry stood behind me on the staircase, laughing, then placed a kiss on my cheek.

We walked into the room together and took our usual seats side by side. We were commencing day two of

Limitations

"Trust", a series of exercises that were supposed to help us not only trust others but trust ourselves. I didn't see much of a point in any of it, but I guess that the decrease in the frequency of my eye rolls at Andrea's words must have meant that we were making some progress at least. The session began with trust falls, an exercise in which we had to fall backwards into a partner's arms and trust them to stop us from hitting the ground. Harry and I had not gotten very far – we had spent most of the allotted time giggling and making fun of each other. Andrea, who kept glaring at us from across the room, had clearly had enough.

"The teams who are not working as well as they should be will be chosen to demonstrate appropriate trust falls to the entire group," Andrea said loudly to the whole group, but it felt like it was intended solely for us.

There was a muffled grunt from Dwayne who had now dropped Aaliyah on the floor seven times. He had continued to try despite Aaliyah's insistence that they switch places or at least take a break.

Pulling myself together, desperate to not be called out again, I nodded to Harry before turning around with my back facing him. I was just about to fall when I heard it. A massive explosion rang through the entire building, glass shattered, and then there were screams, louder than anything I had ever heard. The world around me spun until suddenly ... everything went black. Something thick covered my eyes and entered my lungs. I couldn't see ... I couldn't breathe. I threw my body to the ground and felt everything falling around me.

Chapter 24

When I came to, the oxygen left in the room was almost non-existent. The air felt thick and hot and smelt like metal and smoke. I felt someone violently shaking my body, and I heard Harry screaming, "Lilly, get up! We have to get out of here!"

Shaking, I tried to stand up from my position on the ground, but my body resisted. Through the thick smoke that filled the room, I could see that everyone else had also thrown themselves on the floor. You don't live in America this long and not duck for cover when you hear a noise like that because it usually only means one thing – and it's never good.

"What happened?" I asked, looking around at them all.

Most of them still laid there, their bodies shaking with the weight of fear on top of them.

"I have no idea," Harry said, "but we can't stay here, it isn't safe." He got to his feet, shaking as he did so.

My heart pounded against my chest as I pushed myself to stand. The ground beneath me shook.

"I don't think the floor is stable!" I yelled to Harry. "It feels like it's about to cave in."

In a far-off corner, someone screamed, but I didn't get a chance to work out who it came from before I heard a loud crack. The ground gave way and I felt myself falling rapidly.

I remember reading once that every human is born with a fear of falling. It's an evolutionary predisposition.

Limitations

Studies have shown that babies who have never felt that God-awful dropping feeling before still recognise it as something to be afraid of and will instinctively reach out for something to save them. I guess this explains why I reached out for the snack table to stop me from falling to my death, but it fell right down with me. All around me, there were crashes and dreadful cries of pain, until everything went black once more.

When I came to, the air hitched in my throat, trying and failing to make its way into my lungs – the pain was excruciating. It felt like every single part of my body had shattered into a thousand pieces, which was probably not untrue. The table lay on top of my body, and my clothes were covered in various foods. I managed to fight through extreme chest pain to lift the table off me and push it aside. Now freer to move, I sat up and looked around at the carnage around me, groaning in pain as I did so. The room looked like a scene out of a post-apocalyptic film. Across the space, Dwayne clutched his wrist as he desperately tried to wake Aaliyah up; Grant stared at the opposite wall, looking shell-shocked; and Andrea was face down and seemed to be unconscious, but she was still breathing, judging by the slight rise and fall of her upper back.

"Lilly," a familiar voice groaned.

As I turned toward the sound of the voice, I suddenly saw way more of Harry than I had ever wanted to. Through his now ripped jeans, part of what I assume was his tibia was visible, having stabbed its way through multiple layers of muscle, skin and denim.

"Oh my god, Harry," I yelled, crawling toward him. The ground shook ever-so-slightly. We were not on the bottom floor of the building, and I was not in the mood for another trip downstairs, so I adjusted my body, ensuring my weight was evenly distributed through all four throbbing limbs before continuing to move toward him.

Limitations

"I think my leg is broken," he said, looking straight at me.

"Um ... I don't think you need medical training to guess that," I said, looking around for something or someone who might be able to help. "Do me a favour and don't look down."

"Why not," Harry muttered, lifting the top half of his body to look at his leg. His eyes popped open and his body began to shake. Then he slumped back to his prior position. "Ouch," he said with a shudder.

"Um ... what do I do?" I asked, raking my brain for anything that might be useful, and trying desperately not to think about the possibility that at any minute the entire place could go up in flames or worse.

"You're going to get out of here," said Harry. "That's what you are going to do. Go get help. Tell them where we are. Get yourself to safety." He took my hand in his. His face was screwed up, pain stricken and broken. It sent chills through every part of my body.

"Oh, for god sake, shut up!" I yelled, pulling my hand promptly out of his grip. "We are not doing this. This isn't a movie; we aren't doing the dramatic 'save yourself' speech. You just need a splint. So, I need wood or something like that, right?" I asked, my eyes darting rapidly around the room, looking for something that might help.

Harry let out a loud groan, then slowly drifted off.

"Come on, Harry, now is not the time for a nap. I need you!" I cried, shaking his body. But then I stopped, suddenly realising how much adjusting his leg would hurt him if he were alert – it would be better with him unconscious.

"The table might work," Dwayne said with a strained voice from the other end of the room.

"The table?" I asked.

Limitations

"It's a camping table, I think," said Dwayne with a shake in his voice. "Most of them come apart easily because they're designed to be assembled without the need for tools. I would help, but I think my wrist is broken. Try the legs, and if that works, I can talk you through the rest."

"Ok," I whispered. "You stay put," I said to Harry, despite being certain that he couldn't hear me, then cautiously crawled my way back to the snack table.

Dwayne was right in thinking it would be easy to disassemble the table. The one remaining unbroken leg came out of its socket with a gentle pull.

"Ok, you need to place that behind his leg," Dwayne said, watching me as I fiddled with the table leg. "But do your best not to move his leg at all, and don't push the bone back in – it could cause nerve damage."

I nodded, crawling my way back to Harry with the table leg. "Don't push the bone back in," I whispered softly to myself as if it were the most important thing in the world.

Delicately, I placed the table leg underneath Harry's leg, trying as hard as I could not to move it too much or too suddenly. I lifted his foot slightly to get it in the right place.

Harry jolted back to reality with an ear-piercing scream.

"I'm sorry, I'm sorry, I'm sorry," I whispered, reaching my hand up to hold on to his.

"It's ok," he groaned, squeezing my hand. "What's not ok, is you wasting time helping me when you should be getting to safety," Harry said sternly, his pain evident with every word.

"Oh, shut up, would you!" I heard a voice say from the other side of the room. "We are in this together, remember? We don't leave until we all can." It was Aaliyah. She and the others were watching my efforts as they nursed their own injuries.

"Is there anything we can do, Lilly?" Grant asked. He was visibly shaken but seemed to be uninjured.

Limitations

"Um ... no, it's ok. Look after each other, that's the most important thing," I replied desperately, looking around at all of them.

"What do I do now?" I yelled to Dwayne.

But it was Harry who answered. "You need a bandage," he said. "Some sort of material to wrap around it."

Looking around at the calamity that surrounded us, I scanned for anything that I could use, but the rubble that lined the floor was useless. I suddenly remembered the cardigan I'd thrown in my handbag earlier that morning.

"Can anyone see my handbag?" I yelled. "It's Michael Kors, black and white with a white handle," I explained, glancing around the room as quickly as I possibly could.

"Over here," Grant roared, pulling the bag out from under a mess of broken floorboards.

"Open it up! There's a black cardigan inside," I shouted.

Grant rummaged around in the bag and pulled out the cardigan. He threw it toward me, and I caught it mid-air.

"This might hurt," I whispered to Harry as I began rolling the cardigan into the shape of a bandage.

Harry just took a deep breath in, bit down on his finger and braced for the pain.

As carefully as I could, I began wrapping the cardigan around his leg and the table leg, securing it in place. Harry screamed in pain.

Under my breath, I whispered, "I'm sorry, I'm sorry, I'm sorry," on a loop.

When it was finished, I looked around, waiting for the next piece of advice and desperately wishing I had chosen to read more medical books.

"You need to feel for a pulse," Dwayne spoke up.

"Harry's talking to me!" I snapped. "He's not dead, Dwayne."

Limitations

"In my leg, Lil," Harry whispered. "If there isn't one, it's too tight."

Careful to avoid the broken skin, I placed two fingers on Harry's calf and waited. It took a few moments, but eventually I felt the subtle beat of the blood pumping through his damaged leg. I exhaled with a loud sigh before announcing to the room that there was a pulse.

"So ... what now?" Aaliyah spoke quietly.

"Someone needs to wake the wackadoo up," Dwayne said, looking down at the motionless Andrea whose life was only made known by the dust that became unsettled every time she exhaled.

"Would it be bad if we left her here?" I laughed slightly. Ashamed of myself for even thinking it, I pulled myself together and moved carefully toward her.

Chapter 25

This is it – the worst thing is happening right now. Can you hold it together, Lilly? Or will you crack under the weight of it all? This is the thought that played on repeat in my head.

It took a few minutes and a great lot of poking and prodding to get Andrea to come back around. When she did, she didn't seem terribly aware of where she was; she stared into the distance, dazed and confused.

"Where's Frank?" she asked wearily. "He was supposed to meet me here." I stared around the room ... there was no Frank among us. Andrea looked around, then collapsed back onto the unstable ground.

Limitations

"It's been pretty quiet for a while," Dwayne said as I tried to wake Andrea up again. "Maybe it's safe to just go and get some help and leave the ones who can't walk behind?" he said finally.

The words had no sooner left Dwayne's mouth when we heard it.

My mum and I used to play this game, Fireworks or Gunshots, where we would try to work out the source of the loud cracks that filled the New York City sky each night. It's quite sadistic when you think about it, but it was a way of calming ourselves down. Coming up with a reason that someone might be letting fireworks off made the possibility that we were in danger seem less real. The sound of four loud cracks rang through the building, and I knew immediately that they were not fireworks. In the distance, a faint scream grew louder and louder and louder until it rushed past the closed door and faded once more. Harry's eyes darted from me to the door.

"That can't be a good sign," he whispered.

Two more cracks rang out, closer this time, followed by more ear-piercing screams.

"We can't just sit here. We're sitting ducks," I whispered, searching for a way out.

"There are eleven of us in this room, Lilly," Aaliyah said, shaking as she spoke. "We can't exactly all leave together. It puts even more of a target on our backs."

Trying to build a plan in my head, I looked desperately around the room for something new I hadn't seen the first hundred times I had scanned it.

"Ok ... we'll split up," I delegated to the group, trying with all my might not to let my voice shake. "No one should be alone. And be careful – the shooter could be around any corner."

One by one, members of our group joined up and vigilantly headed off in different directions. Shots continued to ring out in the distance. My heart raced more and more rapidly with each shot, knowing full well it could be any one of our group on the receiving end. Within a few minutes, there was just Harry, myself, Dwayne and Andrea left in the room.

"You guys go," Dwayne said exasperated. "There's no way I'm getting her to come with me, and I'm not going to leave her alone like this. I will stay low and out of sight and hope for the best." He finished with a nod.

"Dwayne …" I whispered, imploring him to reconsider.

"Thank you, Lilly," said Dwayne, "for showing me kindness at a time when I didn't know how to be kind to myself. Thank you for reuniting me with the people I never thought I would be able to show my face around again." He smiled. "I know you set off the fire alarm. Your friend there"—Dwayne pointed at Harry—"was pretty proud. He had to tell me."

I smiled at Dwayne. "Try to stay alive, ok?" I said.

"Always," Dwayne whispered.

Harry stood up, groaning in pain, and leaned on me like a crutch. We stumbled out of the room, down the hallway and towards the same extravagant staircase we had walked up that morning.

A gunshot echoed in the distance. Someone screamed. Harry stopped hopping. A woman ran past, pushing us out of the way.

"Go on without me," said Harry. "I'm just slowing you down."

I whacked him gently on the arm, and then we carried on together, approaching the end of the hallway.

A floorboard creaked. I stopped dead in my tracks.

The small but deadly barrel of a gun poked out from the doorway of the room in front of us.

The gunman.

Harry clutched my waist.

Limitations

The pit of my stomach seemed to fall to my feet. I stared between the stairs and the door, trying to formulate something resembling a plan. If we went down the stairs, we would walk straight past that room, and probably wouldn't live to tell the tale. If we stayed put, we were sitting ducks and, again, probably wouldn't live to tell the tale.

There, beside the stairs, was a door. It was hidden in the dark-coloured wood.

Jumping forward, I opened the door of the storage cupboard and scrambled inside. I pulled Harry in, covering his face with my hand to muffle his screams of pain. I had been told no sudden movements – but in that moment, I had no other choice. After gently closing the door behind us, we sat in the pitch darkness. There was nothing more we could do now. We just had to sit and wait and pray that the shooter hadn't gotten his head around that corner before we closed the door.

Harry was obviously in pain. I could hear him whimpering. His hand gripped my leg tighter and tighter – part of me liked to think that he was making sure I was still there beside him. It was darkness like nothing I had ever experienced. The kind that could drive you completely mad if you sat in it for too long. But we had to just wait it out. Every part of my body burned from the fall. I was running on adrenaline, and my body still hurt more than anything I had ever experienced. I didn't want to stop and fathom what kind of injuries both of us would have to recover from if we ever actually got out alive.

It felt like a lifetime inside that closet before we heard another noise outside. When we did, it was another two gunshots and two loud smashes. Breathing rapidly, I realised that the bullets must have gone through the window, the same window we had just stood in front of ... they were for us. I heard footsteps in the distance, getting closer and closer. I held my breath and gripped Harry's hand, which was resting on my leg. The footsteps stopped, and there was a soft brushing noise on the outside of the closet door. He had found the closet.

This was it. We weren't getting out of this one.

I continued to hold my breath, thinking hard about the days Harry and I spent together on that beach and anything else I could to stop me from screaming out. Tears welled in my eyes as I thought about every opportunity I had not taken – all the years I had wasted suffering in silence, all the things I would not get a chance to do. And then, as if I had willed it so, I heard the footsteps again, slowly but surely fading away until they could no longer be heard.

"Oh, my god," Harry whispered through the blackness.

"I thought we were dead and gone," I whispered, finally allowing myself to breath once more. "How's your leg?"

"We need to get out of here, Lil. We can worry about that later."

I nodded, forgetting that he couldn't see me, and crept forward to open the door to the storage closet.

"You stay put," I said quickly. "I'll help you out when I'm in the hall and can see a bit better."

I crawled my way out of the small doorway, then rose to my feet. I stood up straight, stretched my back out and, without a second thought, bent back down to help Harry out.

I heard him scream before I felt the pain. I felt the pain before I heard the shot. Everything flashed before me. And in an instant, everything went black all over again. I heard a gurgling wheeze in my chest, sirens and heavy footsteps, gunshots, and someone fall to the ground.

Then, like a beacon in the dark, I heard his voice in my ear, "Everything is going to be ok, Lilly. I'm here. It's ok."

Chapter 26

As a kid, I never played video games all that much. If I'm being honest, I was never really any good at them. I always found myself dead long before everyone else or repeatedly turning a wheel, trying to get my car back on track. During one game, I vividly remember crashing my digitally rendered car into the Eiffel Tower eighteen times before it fell down on top of half of Paris. I sometimes think about life in the same way. I'm constantly turning wheels, fiddling with triggers and moving strings behind the scenes, trying to get things back on track. In the end, it's just as futile as trying to get that badly rendered Xbox car out of the muddy pits of the artificial racecourse. And if I am able to get it back on track, what's to stop me from running offcourse again or running out of lives in the only game in which you don't get a second chance?

Since the support group started, every day felt like a video game, an alternate version of reality. And in the instant that bullet hit me, real life came crashing down on me like a thousand bricks, and there was absolutely nothing I could do to stop it. I felt myself run out of lives. In the distance, sirens still rang on. I could hear rushed, panicked voices, but they were too faint to distinguish. On a loop in my head, I saw my mum, laughing with me as we stuffed our face with sweets. I saw Harry, his beautiful smile reminding me of all the good things in this world. I saw Ella, drunk, dancing around a sweaty nightclub like an animal escaped from the zoo. I saw myself, brighter and happier than I ever remember myself being. My heart soared as the images played like a movie in my head.

Limitations

Perhaps this is what happens when you die – all the physical pain fades away, and you are just left with the happy memories, reminders of all the good parts of your life. Or maybe not? Maybe this is the brain switching into fight mode. Maybe it shows you the happy memories and takes the pain away so you have something to fight for.

I knew it would be easier to stay in this pain-free zone, imaging happier moments. It would be kinder to fade away from reality, but I knew that I was stronger than the person I used to be. Something inside me had changed, and I didn't want to just lay down and take it anymore. I wanted to get back up. I wanted to keep fighting. I wanted to be good at the video game – this crazy illusion of life that I only get one shot at. I didn't want to throw it away or give up on it just because someone gave up on me all those years ago. I had no choice but to keep playing, to keep fighting.

In the darkest parts of my mind I saw faces: Harry, Mum, Ella ... then the faces of every single member of that support group, every single person who was brave enough to stand up and fight for their lives. Were they ok? Did they make it out? I chose not to dwell on that for too long, but instead, to let them inspire me. I chose to follow in their lead, to not lay down and die but to stand up and push through.

In the distance, the beeps and sirens got louder. The voices became clearer. I heard my name in the faintest whisper, and then much louder. I heard the words that pierced my heart and soul, "She's lucky to be alive" and for the first time in my life, I believed it.

It must have been hours before I woke up again, but when I did, the agonizing pain had returned. It took a minute for my eyes to adjust and for my head to stop spinning, and I realised that the white light shining down on me wasn't the light that everyone feared. It was just a bright examination light.

Limitations

Harry sat beside me in a designated hospital wheelchair, his leg wrapped in a tight cast. He stared out the window on the other side of the room, and his hand gripped tightly onto my own. I hadn't believed that anything too bad had happened to him because I had felt him beside me most of the time I was out. But seeing him was like a weight being lifted off my shoulders. I breathed a sigh of relief. On the other side on my bed, my mother was sound asleep, her arms wrapped tightly around the t-shirt I'd been wearing that morning. I was now in a hospital gown and draped in multiple layers of hospital blankets. Neither Mum nor Harry knew that I was awake, and for a second I was ok with that. I closed my eyes again and allowed the excruciating pain to overcome my body.

Finally, I whispered Harry's name. My voice came out croaky and it shocked me how much it hurt to breathe a sound.

Harry jumped straight into action, asking if I needed anything, hitting the call button to get a nurse into the room and waking up my mum from her sleep. I squeezed his hand as tightly as I could muster and smiled at him.

Harry told me that he had had surgery to fix his leg. He wouldn't be able to walk on his own for quite some time, but he was on some pretty powerful drugs, and overall, he was ok. Mum told me that they caught the guy who shot me and twenty-four others inside the library and that he was on a one-way trip to prison. They gently tried to explain the extent of my injuries, but, if I'm being honest, I didn't take in too much of what they were saying. It was all too overwhelming, and at that point, all I cared about was that I was alive and Harry was alive, and everything else could be worked out later.

And then I remembered the library, and every single person in that room. Had they made it out? Or had they not been as lucky?

Limitations

"What about ..." I stopped. My lungs ached more and more with every raspy breath.

"Everyone is fine, Lilly," Harry said softly. "You got the worst of all of us, so please rest." He placed a hand on my shoulder, stopping me from getting out of the bed.

I did as he said, giving into the weight of my injuries and laying my head on the pillow. Closing my eyes, I allowed all the pain to fade away. For the first time, I didn't feel like I was fighting a war all on my own. With Harry and Mum by my side, I knew that no matter how hard the next few months would be, I would be ok.

Dear Lilly,

You were shot today. The worst thing, literally, happened, and you are still alive. You have spent your whole adult life thinking that when the worst happens you would suffocate, but you are still breathing - as painful as it may be. Bad things happen. They will happen no matter how long you spend worrying about them. And it isn't always going to be easy to get up the next day, but as long as you are alive, you will make it through. This isn't the end of you - it's just the beginning. There's a long road ahead, but this is step one. Be proud of who you are,

Limitations

stop questioning why your father wasn't,

and get up and fight for your life!

Love Lilly

stop questioning why your father wasn't,

and get up and fight for your life!

Chapter 27

Therapy Log 1:

When the trauma counsellor walked into my hospital room this morning, the old me – the pessimist who believes she's too far gone to benefit from any kind of help – switched back into gear. However, as Julianna sat down next to me, her sweet smile glowing brightly in that dark room, I let my guard down a little. She spoke to me like I was an old friend, and she listened to every seemingly insignificant thing I wanted to say. She gave me a task: after each session I should write a short recap of how I was feeling, any thoughts

Limitations

I had that worry me and how I found the session. So here we go:

I am in a lot of pain. It's only three days post trauma (as Julianna called it) and I haven't spent too long thinking about what happened. I guess, for now, physical pain is taking the driver's seat.

Sometimes I worry that I'm not strong enough to push through the inevitable months of pain that will follow. I worry that my mental health, which is just starting to feel a little more stable, will crumble under the pressure.

It's always hard after the first session, but I don't feel too bad. I feel respected.

Therapy Log 2:

Five days post trauma. Is it possible the pain is getting worse each day? My lung capacity is getting better, but it's still too weak for me to leave the hospital.

I worry that I made the wrong choices in that library. Harry has such a long road to recovery; his nerves are so badly damaged, and I worry that I'm to blame.

Our session today was incredibly productive. I spoke for the first time about what happened in that room. It feels good to open up, just a bit.

Therapy Log 3:

Six days post trauma. My lung capacity is the best it's been. I've been able to sit up regularly in my bed and move around more freely. The pain is still excruciating, but it's slowly getting better.

I heard a car backfire this morning. It was just outside my window. I jumped so fast that the pain of the movement made me scream. I spent the next hour shaking and crying. I wasn't meant to have a session today, but Julianna was forced to come and help me calm down. I called Harry, but he didn't answer. I know now that he was in a physio session. Sometimes I feel like a burden on everyone around me.

Julianna has this unique way of making me feel like I'm the most important person in the universe. I'm sure she does this to every patient, but I never feel like I bother her or that any of my thoughts are irrational around her. She makes me feel like I deserve a safe space.

Therapy Log 4:

Nine days post trauma. My lung capacity is outside of the danger zone and I was released from the hospital this afternoon. I feel a little more human being back home. The pain is still beyond excruciating, but the painkillers help.

Sometimes I worry that I'm not handling this well. I don't spend every second dwelling in the darkness like I thought I would. Most of the time I am bright and bubbly until something drags me down. Is there something wrong with me? Am I too used to pain? Should I be more afraid than I am?

Before I left the hospital, Julianna hugged me and told me that everything would be ok. I will see her again, just less frequently and in a different setting. For the first time in my life, I believe that I might be ok. I have so long to go, but I am stronger than I ever imagined.

Chapter 28

Harry was out of his cast and in a walking boot – to his great

relief – the trips up my stairs on those crutches had been his

least favourite part of the day. He still hobbled his way

around the apartment, but with the help of a great physio

team, walking was getting a lot easier.

Almost every day, Harry had spent time with me as I

recovered from my injuries, either at the hospital or my

apartment where he would go downstairs and bring up piles

and piles of unpublished books for us to read to each other.

We ordered pizza and occasionally made lunch together.

Most importantly, we laughed, as hard as my broken body

would allow. Harry seemed to be becoming quite close with my mother which, if I'm being completely honest, made me uncomfortable.

Ella had also been around quite a few times. On the days that Harry couldn't be there with me, she sat by my bedside, and we talked about anything that might distract me from the pain. We watched TV shows and laughed a lot. On her last visit, she was just about to leave as Harry entered through my front door.

"Take care of your heart, baby girl," Ella whispered, with a not-so-subtle wink.

I smiled back at her and told her that I would, and this time, I meant it.

Harry and I had both decided that we didn't want to be present at the hearing for the man who attacked the library. Instead, we sat around on our phones, waiting for updates, and we cried tears of joy when the man was sentenced to a life in prison. Similarly, we cried together

Limitations

when news broke that the very same coward had taken his own life, only a few days after entering prison. Side by side and with a new lightness in our hearts, we pulled each other through what could have easily been one of the darkest periods of our lives. It's amazing how the worst possible event can become somewhat bearable with the right person by your side … and a lot of counselling.

With seven broken ribs, a fractured collar bone and a punctured lung from a gunshot wound to the chest, it was a good six weeks before I really started to feel like myself again. For the first time since the attack, my first instinct wasn't to reach for the bottle of painkillers that sat on my bedside table. Instead, I reached out for the water that sat next to it and swallowed it alone. Slowly, I pulled myself upwards. Reaching for my phone, I sent a text to Harry who would have already been on his way to our apartment, *Hey, let's get out of this muggy apartment :)*

Harry replied almost immediately, *You up to it?*

If you're willing to help, I think I will be ok, I texted with another smiley face. Then I put my phone back on the bedside table and pulled myself out of bed to get ready.

I pulled out a bright yellow sundress from my cupboard and used the "pick-up and reaching" tool, which had become an extension of my arm, to grab a pair of white Keds from the cupboard floor. Once dressed, I exited my room with my phone in hand. A message from Harry was on the screen, *Always*.

A few minutes later, I was halfway through a banana, when there was a knock on the front door. As quickly as my body would allow, I walked to the door and opened it.

"You look nice," Harry said with a smile. "Did you intentionally try to match your outfit to your breakfast?" he joked.

"Very funny," I said, taking another bite of my banana. "Nothing is going to drag me down today, Harold. I feel alive and I feel good. I haven't taken a single painkiller since lunch yesterday." I smiled, waiting for his praise.

The look that I was met with, however, was not admiration. His face was instantly flooded with fear and hesitation. It was the same way he had looked at me in the hospital, like I was fragile. I didn't like feeling this way. For so long, people expected me to break at any second – I didn't want to feel weak any longer.

As if reading my mind, Harry softened his expression and gently whispered, "Just be careful, ok?"

"Be careful? Of what?" I questioned. "I feel great, man." I boxed the air to show how physically fit I was, then stopped, wincing at a sudden ache in my ribs.

"Be careful of that." He laughed with a look on his face that screamed I told you so.

"Message received," I said softly, placing my hand on my side where the pain had been, and returned to my seat at the kitchen counter to finish my breakfast. I slid another banana across the countertop toward Harry.

"Morning, Harry," Mum called as she made her way through the kitchen in her usual rushed fashion.

"Good morning, Miss Dempsey," Harry called back to her with a charming smile, which was probably 90% of the reason she seemed to like him so much.

"How many times do I have to tell you, dear? Call me Katherine," she said, feigning exasperation.

Harry just smiled at her, and picked up the banana and peeled it.

Mum and I had been through a lot over the last few months, and recently she opened up to me about all her own mental health issues. She had been seeing a psychologist on and off since we first moved to the city, and I had had no idea. She was always so focussed on me that I often assumed she didn't need help, but she had support, every step of the way. In the faint light of my depressing hospital room, she had opened up to me about how, for a long time, she felt like romance was completely off the cards for her because she thought she found the love of her life once, and it had gone up in flames. She knew how relationships ended, so she ended anything that had the potential to turn serious before it had even begun. It sounded awfully familiar. She told me that when I went on my little adventures and ran away, it broke her heart, mostly because she thought that I was leaving her, but also, on another level, because she feared that I was doing the same thing she had done in the wake of her marriage falling apart. Mum and I had always been close – there was never a question about that – but there were fundamental flaws in our relationship that stemmed from a lack of understanding and the completely illogical feeling that we couldn't open up to one another. But in knocking that barrier down, in opening up to one another for the first time in my twenty-five years on this earth, I finally understood her, all of her, and I felt like she understood all of me.

"Any big plans today, you two?" Mum said with a smile as she poured herself a coffee.

"Well, I was thinking we might go out for a little bit," I began apprehensively.

Mum had a look of horror on her face.

"Just to get a bit of sunshine before summer is completely over," I added.

Mum still looked uncertain, but when she looked at Harry, her face seemed to lighten. The two of them exchanged a look of understanding, and she nodded.

"Just be careful," Mum replied.

"You know, I'm getting a lot of that today," I joked. "I will be careful, I promise – I'm just going stir crazy in this house."

Limitations

Mum didn't respond. She simply smiled and picked up her things.

"I'm glad to see you happy, Lilly," she said quickly with a smile before exiting the apartment for work.

The words filled me up inside. She wasn't wrong – I was happy, deliriously so, despite everything that had happened. For the first time, I saw a light at the end of the tunnel, a life where everything from my past pushed me forward instead of pulling me back.

Chapter 29

For a while, I had had a plan for the day, but I'd been desperately waiting to feel well enough to put it into action.

As Harry awkwardly hobbled along beside me toward the subway station, he gave me puzzled glances and, every few minutes, hit me with some variation of the same question: "Where are you taking me?" I liked the sense of adventure that came along with not clueing Harry in on my plan one bit.

Harry's obviously broken leg put us at an advantage on the train. Two NYU students jumped out of their seats, allowing us to sit on a bench-style seat at the side of the carriage. Despite our seated position, the subway quickly became a horrible idea. Trains in New York City travel at about fifty miles per hour, and at that speed, they shake everyone inside like pills in a bottle. My slowly healing ribs were not thanking me for it at all. Harry held my hand as I winced through every bump and turn, and when we finally got off the train, I had never been so thankful to be in Brooklyn in my life.

"You hate Brooklyn," Harry said pointedly. "What are we doing here?"

He was not wrong. We agreed on the first day we met that Brooklyn is without a doubt the worst borough of Manhattan, but I had a plan and we had come this far, so I was sure as hell not clueing him in now.

Harry's face changed slightly as I led him down the same streets he had taken me down the day we first met. I couldn't tell if he had worked out my plan or if he was just reliving that first night.

I finally stopped outside the entrance to the Brooklyn Museum, my smile wide, waiting for him to react.

"The museum? Really?" he replied confused, and if I wasn't mistaken, a little disappointed.

"Hey, you love this stupid museum, and I thought"—I gestured to the museum's entrance—"that it would be nice to see it in daylight. You know, so we can actually speak and not have to worry about being arrested at any minute." My smile diminished slightly.

Harry exhaled, his eyes brightening at my words.

"This is what you do to me, Lill," he said with a relieved laugh. "You get this cheeky smile on your face, and I am expecting to end up soaked in a river or naked in a basement, but it's just the museum."

"If you prefer," I began, with the cheekiest smile I could muster, "you could end up naked in the museum."

Harry looked around quickly, before whispering, "Yeah, because that ended so well last time."

Limitations

He was referring to a week ago, when Mum was at work. We had taken making out way too far and found ourselves at a medical centre giving an agonisingly awkward explanation of what had happened to make my pain so bad that day.

"Good point." I nodded, laughing at the memory.

We walked around the museum hand in hand like we had on that first night. We explored exhibits that held much more significance with the lights on, and I smiled widely every step of the way, listening to Harry's long list of random facts about every section.

In front of an exhibit about the ancient city of Troy, Harry told me that, for many years, the city had only existed in legend, until an archaeological site, which was believed to be Troy, was found on the north-west coast of Turkey. He told me about Helen and Paris whose love was supposedly so powerful that it led to the Trojan War and the fall of Troy. I'd heard the story before, but when I saw the pure joy on his face, I didn't have the heart to tell him. His passion inspired me.

Harry spoke softly, trying not to interrupt a tour guide who was giving his own account of the story. "There has been debate over whether Helen really loved Paris or if Paris just stole her away in the night and held her against her will," he said. "I like to think that they were in love – that their connection was so powerful that it pulled her out of her oppressed relationship with Menelaus and taught her how to stand up for what she wanted, and that Helen defied all conventions of the time by leaving the castle and choosing happiness and love over money, power and status."

I liked Harry's version. There's something about a love that breaks down all borders and conventions that speaks to me. I like to think that Helen was free from her past once she finally escaped the walls that were holding her in.

Limitations

As we moved into the same lit-up room we had entered that first day, I was once again overwhelmed by the brightness of it all. Just as he had done before, Harry guided me to sit on the floor beside him, and we sat there for a while, hand in hand, staring at the stars.

"I think I want to be a trauma surgeon," Harry said suddenly, as if he had started a conversation in his head and accidentally continued it out loud.

"Wow ... are you sure about that?" I asked. "I just mean that it's a lot of ... well ... trauma," I finished, not so happy with my explanation.

Harry was cool, calm and collected when it mattered most. I knew he could be amazing as a trauma surgeon, but what I wasn't sure of was whether he could spend every day faced with cases that were so scarily similar to what his father went through.

Harry looked at me gently, in a way that told me he understood where I was coming from.

"I know it's a big 180, but these last few weeks have shown me that absolutely anything is possible," he said softly, "and rather than running from cases that might remind me of my dad, I think I want to focus on them and use them to honour his memory instead of letting it suffocate me."

Harry amazed me. He had from the first moment we had met, and I knew he would continue to every moment he remained in my life. He had this uniquely beautiful way of seeing and understanding life. He never saw the world as black and white. He saw the in-between parts where sun shone through the cracks, illuminating the darkness. He understood that everything in life was connected, and he never lost hope or faith in that. Instead, he used it as a driving force in his life, something that always kept him moving.

"You're going to be an amazing doctor. I hope you know that," I replied with a soft smile, and I really meant it.

Limitations

He cared on a level that I didn't know was even possible before meeting him. I had never met another person more suited for the profession than he was.

"I really hope so," he said, returning my smile.

"I have some news too," I whispered, picking up and shredding an old ticket from the ground.

Harry looked at me intently and reached over to take the ticket out of my destructive hands.

"What did that ticket ever do to you?" he asked.

I stayed silent, staring at the space between my hands where the ticket had been.

"What's your news?" Harry asked.

"I've been writing, like a lot of writing, in any spare minute. I'm not done yet, not even close, but I want to tell this story. The story of the support group, and coming to terms with who I am and learning to be better. And meeting you ... I really hope you're ok with that?" I replied with a whisper. I had written so much about him, and it wasn't until this very moment that it occurred to me that he may not be ok with that.

Harry didn't say anything at first. Instead, he looked straight up into the twinkling stars that illuminated the false sky above us, and I watched as he took a deep and shaky breath.

"Am I a good guy in this story?" he finally asked with one raised eyebrow.

"The best guy," I replied with a gentle smile.

"Then I'm ok with it," he whispered, "and I'm also insanely proud of you. I hope you know that."

Harry embraced me in a hug that felt like both the best thing in the world and then, suddenly, the worst thing, as my chest started to burn from the added pressure.

"Ouch," I muttered softly. Harry quickly released my body with several quick apologies. I smiled at him, letting him know that I was ok.

Limitations

"It took a lot to do this," I said softly, "but after everything that has happened, it suddenly feels like anything is possible – it's not me against the world anymore. I feel like I can take on anything life throws at me and be ok."

"I know you can ... the things you did that day … I could never have even thought about them, let alone put them into action. You are the strongest person I know, even if you don't always believe it yourself." He smiled.

Letting his words fill me up, I looked up at the stars and took everything in with a smile. It felt good to know that he was proud of me, but what felt even better was that I was proud of myself – suddenly, I realised that that was all I had ever needed.

With a deep breath, I turned my attention back to Harry and whispered the three words I had been too scared to say for most of my life, "I love you."

Harry looked shocked but not annoyed or confused. I could see him processing, and as he did, the smile on his face became more and more prominent. The words seemed

to brighten up his already illuminated face.

"I love you so much, Lilly," he replied before

leaning in and placing a gentle kiss on my lips.

Chapter 30

It was two whole weeks later that I found myself sitting on the train, heading to the same train station I had gone to that fateful day. Inside the pit of my stomach, it felt like a tiny demon was doing backflips over and over again until I felt sick. My sweaty hands left tiny wet marks on my jeans where I'd been drying them every few minutes. I fiddled with my hair and tried to imagine I was somewhere I felt safer. Writing, trauma counselling and self-reflection can only prepare you so well to return to the scene of the worst day of your life.

When I got off the train, I followed the same path I always had, but this time, I walked past the library. The doors and windows were still boarded up and police tape lined its perimeters. Sadistic tourists looked on in amazement, taking photos and muttering to themselves. I rolled my eyes at them as I walked past, then checked my phone to be sure I was heading to the right place. The new venue for the reunion day of our program was inside a small office building in the next block over from the library. I paused for a second in the doorway to the new space. The room was much brighter than the old one and didn't fill me with the same sense of impending doom. My eyes immediately caught Harry's who flashed a smile in my direction and beckoned for me to sit beside him. As I walked in, I noticed another snack table in the corner with all the same snacks on display.

We watched and joked together as each member walked into the room. Dwayne and Aaliyah were the last two to enter, their hands intertwined as they took the remaining two seats next to one another. I shot Harry a look of surprise.

Andrea looked battered, like she'd lost a war, but she seemed, never-the-less determined to get started. She stood to commence the session, her whole body appeared to shake under the weight of her thoughts, her eyes looked heavy, like she hadn't slept since the attack. It shocked me at first, until I realised that there was every possibility that that was true. You tend to think of people in her position as being immune to trauma, but the reality is, she has been going through the same pain as each and every one of us over the last few weeks.

"I'm not going to pretend that nothing happened the last time we met"—Andrea's voice shook with every word, her eyes darted around the room as if on high alert—"and I'm not going to act like I'm coping as well as I would like to be."

I felt the turning in my stomach resume.

"What happened to every single one of us was a horrible turn of fate and the irony of a group of our nature getting caught in an attack like that is not lost on me," said Andrea. "Trauma is something I've spent my whole life teaching other people to overcome, but I see now that a degree only takes you so far. It's not as simple as I always believed it to be. We are lucky to be alive, and sometimes that is enough to put the soul at rest. Sometimes, in the worst of times, it's enough to know that you get to wake up and see the sunrise tomorrow. Likewise, sometimes, it is this knowledge, that can be your undoing. Sometimes, the thought that you have to wake up and live in a world where planes just fly into buildings and gunmen kill twenty-four people in a public library breaks you more than witnessing it," Andrea said shakily.

For the first time since we had met, Andrea spoke from the heart, and every single one of us listened intently.

Limitations

"Given everything that we have all been through," she said. "I fail to see how a few trust falls and deflection exercises are going to help any of us. So, instead, I want to hear from you. I want to hear what you've been doing, how you've been coping and what you feel has changed for you since the attack. One of you has been in contact with me, and I think I will let her start," Andrea finished with a nod in my direction.

Beside me, I felt Harry's bemusement as he turned his body to look at me. I chose to ignore whatever bewildered expression he had, and instead, pulled my notebook out of my bag and opened it to the bookmarked page.

"Hi all," I started, looking around the room. "I know that I'm no expert on any of this, but there are a few things that I wanted to say, and I felt like there was no better time to say them. So, I got in touch with Andrea and, well, here we are." I smiled at them all.

In the pit of my stomach, the backflips continued. The air around me got warmer, and as I closed my eyes and took a minute to breath, I felt the darkness threatening to overcome me. But as I opened my eyes again, my whole body absorbed the sunlight that shone brightly into the room through its large windows. I opened my mouth, and with the same force that had held me back so much in the past, I let every word pour out of me.

"I don't want to pretend that my mental state is perfect because it's not. There are days when I wake up and jump out of bed, ready to face the day, fully embracing all the opportunities that I'm so blessed with. But there are also days when I want to stay in bed, sinking deeper and deeper into the sheets, as my body, mind and soul crumbles into the dusty old mattress. Those days, I pretend that the world around me doesn't exist and that I don't exist within it. I don't like to openly share those days with anyone, not even those inside this room whom I have come to love so much."

Limitations

I nodded slightly to Harry, trying desperately to hold back the tears threatening to break through.

"But I know now that they are all a part of my story. It is the good days that give me the strength to push through the harder ones and the bad days that remind me to make the most of the good. Each and every one of you decided to push through a bad day, to share the most damaged piece of your heart with a group of total strangers. You stood up and said that you weren't going to let the awful things that have happened stop you from living your life, and I admire you all so much for it. I admit that I felt like I didn't belong here in the early days. I was so far away when it all happened. I wasn't directly impacted like so many of you were, and I felt like you all knew it. But each of you welcomed me with open arms, and you didn't give up on me – for that, I'm so incredibly thankful. Each of you has shown me that I'm not alone, and I think that's all anyone ever wants to feel."

I wiped the tears sliding down my cheek.

"When I think of what we did, just a mere eight weeks ago – how we came together, how we overcame so many obstacles to save each other's lives – I am overwhelmed with pride. We proved to ourselves, and to each other, that this attack, and the one that came before, do not define who we are. They do not define our mental state and they do not define how we choose to face each day. We stand united, a force to be reckoned with, in the face of terror. We move into our future, telling the world that we are prepared for whatever it might throw at us. We may not be in control, we may need to accept that sometimes things will throw us off guard and that certain days will be harder than others, but we will always get through them. There is always a light shining bright at the end of the tunnel. For me, that light was ignited by each and every one of you inside this room. It stays alight through my fight for my mental health. And that fight doesn't always mean standing up and running toward the swinging range of a gun-wielding maniac.

Limitations

Sometimes that fight is just lying in bed and telling myself that it will get better, and that tomorrow is another day, another opportunity to seize the moment and to take full advantage of the life I've been blessed with. My mental health issues are what put me in this room, but the strength, the courage, the compassion and the resilience in each of you are what kept me coming back and are what will allow me to go forth and live my life. September 11th, 2001 broke every single little piece of me, reshaping me into the mess who entered this room on day one of this program. But moving forward, I will not let it limit the life I lead."

When I finally stopped speaking, I looked up from my piece of paper, and every single person in the room had a tear in their eye, every single person looked broken but strong, defiant and ready to take on whatever came next.

"Jesus, isn't it a bit early in the session to start making us cry, Lilly," India whispered softly.

We all laughed, and then, as if someone had injected a thought in all our heads simultaneously, we stopped and smiled at one another. There truly was nothing we couldn't do.

Chapter 31

As Harry and I walked out of the support group for the final time, I felt the strangest sense of peace. My body still ached with sudden movements, but my heart felt lighter than it had since I was five years old.

We said goodbye to the rest of the group, vowing to meet up again soon, and walked together toward Central Park.

"How come you didn't tell me you were going to do that today," Harry asked softly, his finger brushing the back of my hand as we walked.

"I only decided yesterday. I wanted to share some of the more inspirational thoughts I had had. They have really helped me, and I thought they could help everyone else," I replied. "It has been insanely cathartic writing all of this down," I added with a laugh.

"I'm not at all surprised it was cathartic, Lilly. You have an eye for the written word, and I can't wait to see what you do with that talent. I would also recommend going through some of your old letters. I think you might find some inspiration there," he replied with a cheeky smile.

I smiled, squeezed his hand, and kept walking by his side.

The sun was burning hot in the early afternoon sky as we sat down on a park bench in the crowded Central Park.

I looked up and smiled at two birds flying playfully around one another. In an instant, I remembered a string of words from one of the unpublished books I had read before

Limitations

all of this began: "In the darkest part of the night, you are where I find my light."

*

When I arrived home later that day, I pulled out my laptop and opened my manuscript, taking a moment to read over what I had written so far. I looked across my room to the box of old letters that still sat half-opened near my closet. Placing my laptop on my bed, I moved toward the box and shuffled through the filed letters until I found one in a brown envelope. Every letter had been written on white paper, which I folded or placed in a white envelope. I don't remember ever using a brown envelope. I picked it up and opened it. The writing inside was not my own. My heart stopped as I read the first line.

Dear Lilly,

You are going to hate me for reading these. I know that, but once I started, I just couldn't stop. I am writing this in the hope that one day in the future you will be reading through your old letters, and amongst all the negativity and darkness you have created with your beautiful mind, you might find a little bit of light. I hope that when that day comes, that I am not a long-lost memory. I hope you will read this and smile before calling me up so we can laugh about it together.

As I write this, you are on a plane on your way to Jamaica. Your audacity both humours me and scares the living hell out of me. You said you wanted to run away from it all. I just didn't believe you would do it.

Limitations

There are a million things I wish I could say to you out loud, but as the old expression goes "writing is closer to thinking than speaking", so here goes nothing. First and foremost, I want to say that I am sorry – it was beyond wrong of me to tear down your dreams and try to replace them with my own harsh reality. I want you to know that I will never, in my wildest dreams, even consider doing that to you again.

In your letters you call yourself weak, but when I look at you, I see one of the strongest people I have ever had the pleasure of knowing. You call yourself stupid, but you think in a way that proves exactly the opposite. You act like you have not found your calling in life, and all the while you are using your calling to express this very notion. You are so beautiful. There are not enough words in the English language to describe all the ways you shine. I just wish you could see yourself in the same way that I see you. If you could, maybe you would realise just how perfect you are. Maybe you would see that behind all the fear and insecurity is a gorgeous, young, talented woman desperate to break out into the world.

I want to tell you that when I leave you at the end of each day, I miss you and spend hours thinking of all the things we could do together. I want to tell you that knowing you have run away to find solace rather than running to me leaves a hole right in the centre of my heart. But most of all, I want to tell you that even after only a few short days, I love you more than life itself. I never understood how people said, "I have loved you all

Limitations

my life" when they had only known each other for a few short moments. I understand now – true love is the kind of love you slip into so subtly you almost don't notice it's happening. In these rare moments, you truly feel like you have loved them all your life, and you, my dear, are that kind of love. I have loved you all my life and will love you every day until I leave it.

I am coming to find you. Though by the time you read this letter, you will probably already know that. I pray that when we meet, you don't push me away but let me stay by your side as you come to realise just how brilliant you truly are.

I leave you with a quote from one of the many books on your bookshelf: "Thinking back on it, it's hard to imagine a time when I wasn't hopelessly in love with you."

I will see you soon, my love, where the sky meets the sea.

Yours forever,

Harry

By the time I finished reading, tears were streaming down my face, and I didn't have any hope in the world of stopping them. I stood up and ran to get my phone from my bed. I unlocked it and dialled his number without a second thought. I knew he was at work this afternoon but prayed that he would answer.

"Did you find it?"

"I love you so much," I replied.

Limitations

"I love you under stars and on sandy white beaches," said Harry, "but I also love you in dusty storage rooms, hospital beds and trapped under the rubble of falling buildings," he replied softly. "But I am at work, so I really do have to go. I love you so much. Never doubt yourself, ok?" he added before quickly hanging up his phone.

I moved back toward my desk and looked down at the letter with a smile on my face and a warmth in my heart that spread through my entire body. Silently, I picked up a stick of blue tac off the desk and stuck the letter onto my bedroom wall beside a photo of the two of us rowing boats in Central Park.

Epilogue

Dear Reader,

Two years ago, my life could have ended – hell – it very nearly did. But today, I stand strong, fully recovered and about to head into one of the most important days of my entire life. It's taken a lot of hard work to get to this place.

Limitations

A few weeks after the support group ended, I was speaking to Harry about his decision to become a trauma surgeon - a decision that has just landed him a spot in the intern program at New York Presbyterian Hospital. He mentioned something about how many stories don't get told because they are cut too short and how he wanted to play a part in keeping those stories going, and with that, something in me clicked. My life's purpose, the very thing I was put on this earth to do, had been right under my apartment all this time. So, I started on a journey to contact every single one of those unpublished authors to get their permission to share their stories. Then India, who turned out to be a talented up-and-coming software developer, and I developed an app where unknown authors could have their voices heard. "Unspoken" launches today, and as I write this, I am getting ready to head to the launch party. The first story to launch will be my own, the story of a crazy girl who lost her mind for twenty-four years and, with a lot of help, finally found her way in her twenty-fifth. It will be followed by every single one of the stories I found in that basement and will hopefully become a platform for new authors who don't have one million followers on Instagram

Limitations

but do have a beautiful written voice and an incredible story to tell.

This isn't a story about a girl who is saved by a boy. However, I won't pretend that I don't owe so much to my gorgeous fiancé, and I will spend every damn day thanking him for holding my hand through some of the worst parts of my life.

Every day that we choose to love another person is a day we open ourselves up to the fear and pain of potentially losing them. But does that mean it is better to not love at all? Or is life just about finding the love that makes all that worthwhile? I like to think it's the latter.

I don't have all the answers and I'm not going to pretend that all my problems are magically over. Even a whole two years later that is far from the case. What I do know for sure is that there is so much more out there for me, and I intend to spend every second of it making up for all the time I wasted living in fear or sorrow.

In my recovery, I have learnt that, sometimes, the inconceivable happens and there is nothing you can do to stop or prevent that. But when it does, it's ok to break, it's ok to cry for weeks on end if you need to. But one day, you might feel a bit stronger, and on that day, you need to get back up off the floor; you need to keep on living. It's never the same knowing that the once inconceivable is your reality, but it will be ok. I also learnt that deep down there was nothing wrong with me. I was just a scared little girl who is only now learning to deal with emotions that were too big for a five-year-old.

The most important thing I have learnt since all of this started is that it's ok to not be. Right now, I am happy. I know that in a few days I could wake up and not want to get out of bed, and that is ok too. Because any day that I wake up and get to see the sun rising is another day to heal and another day that I get to be alive – for now, that alone is enough.

Love always,

Lilly

Acknowledgements

I can't believe that after five years of writing, editing, writing again and a hell of a lot of procrastination this book is finally finished. The journey to get to a place where I was ready to self-publish was anything but an easy one but now I am here, I am so blessed for so many people who have pulled me through.

Firstly, to my incredible mother, Lisa. My Mum has been my biggest supporter and a built in best friend since the day I was born. Behind every crazy venture is my mother, pushing me to keep working and keep fighting for what I want. I love you more than life itself Mumma, always remember that, I owe everything I have and am to you.

Secondly, to my Dad. My father is always the last to hear about anything. While my Mum was the first litmus test for the idea that formed this novel, my Dad only a year ago found out I was even writing one. That being said, he was instantly supportive and hasn't doubted me for a minute. Thank you for everything Dad.

To my Nan, I am not sure you will like this book, it's definitely not your usual genre but that's ok. Thank you for fostering my love for reading, for pushing me to be better that I was and for never letting me give up, even when you didn't understand my path in life.

To my Pop, who I pray can read this from somewhere beyond. I am devastated that you never got a chance to read what I am proudest of but I know that you were proud of

anything I did. I love you, I miss you and I will never forget
you.

To my best friend and travel companion Charli, thank you
for supporting me through every heartbreak, for listening to
my nonsense and for bringing light into every dark situation.
Ella is for you, I hope you love her as much as I do.

Lastly, I want to 'thank' those who taught me heartbreak.
Without you I wouldn't be in the place I am now – you
know that place you said I'd never be? Huh, look at that. I
hope you got your peaceful life, I'm going to relish every
minute of the sheer chaos that is this beautiful life.

There's someone else who I want to thank, but he shall
remain nameless for now- maybe one day I'll let him know
that he was such a huge inspiration behind the person that

Harry is. Thank you, unnamed person, for reminding me that life is short, and that it's ok to live it on your own terms.

I also want to thank each and every one of you who has taken the time to read this story. Limitations is so deeply personal and the thought of sharing it with the world has plagued my mind in the lead up to this release. I hope you got out of this book all the things I wanted you to. I hope that when you read this, you are reminded to keep fighting for your life because you are more than the sum of the things that happened to you.

A large part of this book was crafted in lockdown, a time where I really started to understand just how important living is. Anyone who knows me well knows I have a horrible fear of dying but, in writing this book, I have come to learn that the only thing worse that dying is dying before you really got the chance to live… I'll carry that with me for

the rest of my life.

355

This is the end of Lilly and Harry's story but there is more to

come from me as an author. I hope that when that time

comes, you will choose to come with me on that journey.

Aimee J Edwards

Author Bio

Aimee J Edwards grew up in Sydney and Wollongong, Australia. She attended Western Sydney University and obtained a Masters in Creative Writing from Macquarie University. Aimee has been writing and creating stories from a very young age and is so excited to finally be able to share these with the world. Limitations is Aimee's debut novel.

Facebook: https://www.facebook.com/aimeejedwards19

Instagram: https://www.instagram.com/aimeejean1904/

Contact Email: aimee@aimeejedwards.com